TEMPTATION AND THE ARTIST

Gentlemen of Pleasure, Book 2

Mary Lancaster

ARE YOU SIGNED UP FOR DRAGONBLADE'S BLOG?

You'll get the latest news and information on exclusive giveaways, exclusive excerpts, coming releases, sales, free books, cover reveals and more.

Check out our complete list of authors, too!

No spam, no junk. That's a promise!

Sign Up Here

www.dragonbladepublishing.com

Dearest Reader;

Thank you for your support of a small press. At Dragonblade Publishing, we strive to bring you the highest quality Historical Romance from some of the best authors in the business. Without your support, there is no 'us', so we sincerely hope you adore these stories and find some new favorite authors along the way.

Happy Reading!

CEO, Dragonblade Publishing

Additional Dragonblade books by Author Mary Lancaster

Gentlemen of Pleasure
The Devil and the Viscount (Book 1)
Temptation and the Artist (Book 2)
Sin and the Soldier (Book 3)
Debauchery and the Earl (Book 4)

Pleasure Garden Series
Unmasking the Hero (Book 1)
Unmasking Deception (Book 2)
Unmasking Sin (Book 3)
Unmasking the Duke (Book 4)
Unmasking the Thief (Book 5)

Crime & Passion Series
Mysterious Lover
Letters to a Lover
Dangerous Lover

The Husband Dilemma Series
How to Fool a Duke

Season of Scandal Series
Pursued by the Rake
Abandoned to the Prodigal
Married to the Rogue
Unmasked by her Lover

Imperial Season Series
Vienna Waltz
Vienna Woods
Vienna Dawn

CHAPTER ONE

H E SAT IN the rose garden, surrounded by beautiful women. And he took her breath away.

Aline always found her reaction to Stephen Dornan inexplicable. Of course, he was handsome, in a dark yet subtle and refined sort of way. But Aline tended to favor fair men with larger-than-life characters. Mr. Dornan was quiet, almost diffident, and generally too distracted to make conversation, let alone flirt. And yet each time she saw him, her heart skipped a beat, and the air left her lungs.

He had a rare smile like sunshine, which was evident now as one of the women spoke to him. He gazed directly into her face, and Aline knew an unusual twinge of jealousy. Only once had she been aware of him looking at her with such concentration—at Dearham Abbey. She had thought he was sketching her at the time, though there had been no portrait of her among those he had displayed at the Abbey that Christmas.

Forcing herself to walk on after her involuntary pause, Aline surveyed his companions, all bright colors and beauty, like so many butterflies. She would have thought them courtesans, except Mr. Dornan was surely too pure to associate with such. No, these women were artists' models—at least to him.

As she drew closer, she saw that he was indeed sketching. The pencil, like an extension of his long, clever fingers, flew across the book, which he had propped against his knee, deft and sure. The pencil paused, then, with a paper knife he took from his pocket, he cut the page from the book and laid it on the table in front of the girl he had smiled at. While she gazed at it in some awe, he turned to the girl nearest him, asking her something. While she chattered, he watched her, and Aline watched him.

Until—perhaps she blocked some light or shadow from where he needed it to fall—he glanced up and saw her. He looked gratifyingly startled and sprang to his feet.

"Mr. Dornan among the roses," she drawled. "I wish my own talent was up to painting such a scene." She stretched out one languid hand as he moved toward her.

"Princess," he murmured, taking her gloved fingers and bowing over them. When he released her, there were grey-black fingerprints on her gloves. He frowned. "Sorry."

"You are clearly busy, so don't let me disturb you."

"I'm looking for models for a series of paintings," he said. "Some of which will have the background of the pleasure gardens."

Aline's raised her brows. "Paintings of *all* of these ladies?"

"Oh. No. The sketches were a lure to get them here so that I could choose."

Her lips twitched, and his gaze dropped to them. Her stomach fluttered. "Very astute," she managed.

His gaze returned to her eyes. "I thought so. At the time. What brings you here?"

"A card party last evening, believe it or not. But Renwick's Hotel is so comfortable, I have decided to stay a few days."

"Mama!" came her son's happy voice, and she turned to see him rushing toward her, a large tutor striding along beside him. "There are *huge* men, tall as giants!"

"Really? That I *must* see." She swung back to Mr. Dornan and found him watching her intently.

"This is your son?" he said.

For a moment, she hesitated, but Basil had already called her

2

mama, and Dornan, was, after all, a friend of Johnny's. "Yes, this is Basil, and his tutor, Mr. Flowers. Basil, make your bow to Mr. Dornan."

Basil, growing into a long-legged eight years old, bowed correctly. "How do you do, sir?"

"I'm very pleased to meet you," Dornan replied and exchanged nods with Mr. Flowers. "You are enjoying the pleasure gardens?"

"Oh, yes, it was a great idea of Mama's to come here."

"I beg you won't tell anyone," Aline said lightly. "I can't have polite society thinking I embrace such unfashionable pleasures. We'll leave you to your sketches, Mr. Dornan. Good morning."

STEPHEN DORNAN SAT down and tried to recall which girl he had been sketching. The last one, thank God. It was an effort to concentrate when his mind was full of another face, another idea that was carrying him away with the kind of eagerness that seemed to surge up from his belly. Only his best ideas affected him thus, though there were no guarantees he could execute this one. Or that she would agree.

She. Aline. Princess Hagerin. Twice widowed that he knew of and once the lover of his friend Johnny Winter. At Dearham Abbey, he had *ached* to paint her. And more. He had dared only a sketch, which had done her such poor justice that he had never shown it. As for the *more*… She was well above his touch.

Handing out the last sketch, he said politely, "Thank you, ladies. I will be in touch when I see my way clear. I appreciate your company." Rising, he bowed and strode off in the direction he had last seen Aline. He was vaguely aware of the rise of confused conversation behind him but kept moving until he found the men on stilts and jugglers who were entertaining people up and down one of the main paths.

However, he could see no sign of Aline or the boy or even his extremely large tutor. They must have moved on to other delights, like the castle or the waterfall or a large plate of ices. Maida Pleasure Gardens, in daytime, was an innocent, if slightly faded, joy for children. And adults, if looked upon correctly.

He could trail around the garden looking for them. But she had said they were staying at Renwick's, the new hotel built on the edge of the grounds. So, he made his way directly there instead, asked the doorman if Princess Hagerin had returned, and, discovering she had not, deposited himself in the nearest sofa to wait. Crossing one ankle over the other knee, he got out his pencil and sketchbook and began sketching from memory, trying to capture the expressions that turned prettiness into beauty and fired his artistic imagination.

He separated her features, showing only her eyes and brows when she was being provocative—"*Mr. Dornan among the roses,*" indeed!—and when she was genuinely amused, and then when she looked at her son. Beneath all the beguiling, long-lashed, almond-shaped eyes, which weren't quite right although they were close, he drew a series of lips as part of the same expression. Her lips obsessed him, their full yet delicate shape and the way the corners quirked very slightly upward. Her mouth could often be serious while her eyes laughed. And he had seen her smile while her eyes turned bleak.

She was the most fascinating woman he had ever encountered, and if she allowed him the right to *try* to capture that on canvas...

It was her scent that roused him, as he had known it would. A hint of lime and hyacinth and some elusive spice—sophisticated, provocative, and lovely, like the lady herself. She entered the foyer, smiling at her son's chatter, the tutor trailing behind. Since her golden blonde head was turned in his direction, it was inevitable that she saw him.

Her smile froze for the tiniest instant. Probably, she did not care to be pursued by him, or by anyone when her son was with her.

He rose and bowed. "Princess. Could you spare me a moment of your time?"

There was a pause, and his heart sank. She was going to deny him and his all-consuming idea would be strangled at birth. It would not work with another woman.

"Fortunately, I can, since it is lesson time once more. Cake for tea, Basil, if Mr. Flowers is pleased with you."

Basil opened his mouth to protest, then appeared to think better of it and smiled instead, offering Stephen a wave as he trotted away beside the tutor.

The princess sat at the end of the sofa and gestured with one hand to invite Stephen to the other. He sat, turning to face her, holding the hastily closed sketchbook on his lap.

"Madame la princesse," he began, since this was how he always thought of her. "I have a proposition to lay before you."

"Why, Mr. Dornan, I am surprised at you," she drawled.

"No, you are not, and you know perfectly well I would never presume."

"On the contrary, sir, I know you so little I have no idea what you might presume."

"Nothing improper," he assured her before honesty compelled him to admit, "Nothing *very* improper."

"Be still, my beating heart," she murmured.

Stephen knew when he was being teased, even subtly. There would be time, later, if she agreed, for him to give as good as he got, but for now, he needed her simply to agree. "I mentioned to you the series of paintings on which I need to embark. It is for a new competition to be held in Paris later this year, a judgment of skill to be made via a series of paintings—no fewer than three, no more than six—that must somehow be linked or related to each other.

"My original idea—because I love the changing light, the color, and the atmospheres of Maida—was to paint a series of women in the rose garden at various times of the day, all behaving differently to display a whole spectrum of…womanhood. At work, nurturing, laughing, flirting."

"Hence the harem in the rose garden," she murmured. "Why women?"

"A good question. There is a cynical aspect. For me—and for the men who will judge the paintings, for the most part – they will be pleasanter to look at. And on a deeper level, women fascinate me. Men are vaunted as the stronger sex, but most of us lack the inner strength of most women, who need, often to survive, to be all things to all people. I wanted to show that strength, that drudgery and hardship and laughing good spirits among the beauty of the rose garden. Which itself is subject to the changes of the seasons."

Curiosity entered her brilliant eyes. "That is surprisingly…profound."

"I thought so. And with some of the women…you saw, I think, I could have made it work quite well. And then I saw you."

Was that alarm behind her suddenly veiled eyes? Suspicion?

"What would I be?" she mused, her voice light, and yet he suspected her mood was anything but. "Not the coquette, for I am beyond such immaturity. The fallen woman, perhaps? The siren?"

"You misunderstand me. I do not judge you, and if I did, it would hardly be in such terms. I see beauty, character, a woman who has created and endured much in her life, a mother, a lady full of life and laughter and sadness." He paused as her eyes narrowed.

"Do you?" she said after a moment.

"For a beginning. When we met in the garden, I suddenly saw in you *everything* I had been looking for, and another idea took hold of me. To paint the *same* woman in all her many roles."

Her eyes widened. For a moment, she said nothing, then, "Would that not be a bit dull? Just portrait after portrait of me in the rose garden?"

"To make that work, I would have to abandon subtlety, so,

no. I would like to paint you in the rose garden in the morning, and perhaps in the moonlight. But also, indoors. With your son, if you will allow it. I can't tell until I begin." He drew a deep breath. "Will you agree to sit for me?"

Her gaze dropped from his to her hands, looking perhaps at the fingerprints he had marked on her gloves. She glanced back up, searching his face, her expression carefully veiled. A pulse throbbed subtly at the base of her throat. He had no idea what that meant, although he knew a powerful urge to feel the vibration against his fingertips, his lips.

"I cannot sit all day, every day," she said. "I would go mad and so would Basil."

"I would not ask that of you."

A smile flickered across her lips. It did touch her eyes, too, though its meaning was well concealed. She personified the mystery of womanhood, and that excited him on every level from the purely intellectual to the artistic to the basely physical. As for his imagination...

"Then I agree. When do we begin?"

"Now, if you wish."

She blinked, and he gave her a rueful smile.

"Which is where the slight impropriety sneaks in," he admitted. "I could begin my sketches here or in the gardens, but I think we would both be distracted by the curious. And if our conversation is easily overheard, I will never get to know you."

"You want to get to know me?" She sounded startled.

"I need to. If I am to see you as you are."

"Are all artists so thorough?" she asked at last.

He shrugged. "A fleeting expression can be enough. It depends on the project. For mine...the paintings will be a *study* rather than the capture of a moment. Is that a problem?"

"I don't know."

"I will not ask impertinent questions or pry. It is *you* I wish to know, not what you have done."

"Are the two not connected?"

"Perhaps. But whatever you tell me is obviously up to you."

"It is what you see without my telling you that worries me."

"I never realized you were afraid." The words were out as he thought them, and he could not take them back.

Her eyes flashed. Her chin lifted. But she said only, "Everyone is afraid. Of something. Aren't you, Mr. Dornan?" She stood, obliging him to rise with her.

"Yes," he admitted.

"Then, on that understanding, we shall proceed. You may take me where you will."

"YOU MAY TAKE me where you will." It was, of course, a stupid thing to say, but around Dornan, she always seemed to have an irresistible urge to shock. Or just to make him notice her. Today, such tactics were quite unnecessary, for he suddenly *had* noticed her—and above the bevy of beauties surrounding him earlier in the rose garden.

And in any case, he only offered his arm in his usual polite, patient manner and led her to the staircase. He was a man comfortable with saying nothing, and she refused to fill the silence with questions or small talk that might make her appear more nervous than she was. Not that she feared Stephen Dornan.

He led her along the second-floor passage and around the corner to where four steps led to the doors to the staff staircase. To the right of the four steps, was another door which Aline imagined led to a cupboard. But it was to this door he applied his key and ushered her inside.

On the threshold she paused. "Well, I did say take me where you will. Somehow, I never imagined it would be to your bedchamber."

"Look on it as my studio," he said. "If you don't mind. Perhaps, if your own rooms include a sitting room, you might be more comfortable there."

"They don't." She lied from instinct because it intrigued her to be here. She walked in, gazing around her.

The room was at the back of the hotel, in a column that jutted out from the main structure of the building, so that it had windows on three sides. Apart from the furniture—bed, bedside cabinet, dressing table and wardrobe, a small desk, chair, sofa, table—a trunk full of paints, canvases, brushes, and other accoutrements sat open under one window. Several easels were piled in the corner.

"You chose it for the light," she guessed. "Even though you planned to be painting in the gardens."

"I am always working on something."

"I noticed that at Dearham Abbey."

His quick glance seemed to denote surprise. Why? That she had noticed him? She almost laughed.

"Make yourself comfortable," he invited. "Shall I fetch us tea? A glass of wine?"

"Wine would be pleasant," she said boldly. "Although I have to point out that if you pull that bell beside you, a hotel servant will take your order."

"And bring it. I thought you might prefer not to be seen here."

"Mr. Discretion," she mocked, but he was already gone, leaving her to take off her gloves, bonnet, and light pelisse. Since there was an empty hook on the door, she hung them there, then wandered around the room.

It seemed he had just arrived, for an open bag of clothing lay on the bed. She itched to shake them out and put them away in his wardrobe. Since it was hardly her place, she refrained, although she did sit on the bed and with a spurt of amused guilt, bent and sniffed the black coat at the top of the bag. She smiled because it smelled very faintly of him. Not paint, but soap, she thought, pleasantly earthy and overall warm and masculine. Enough to encourage the butterflies which had grown quiet in his absence.

She rose quickly and wandered to the window near the desk. His sketchbook lay there, tempting her. He had been drawing in it when she had entered the hotel. Had he been sketching a likeness of her? After all, he had waited to approach her, after abandoning all his eager beauties in the garden.

She snatched back her reaching hand. It felt too much like spying, and she wanted Stephen Dornan to be her friend. Pathetically enough. So, she admired the view from the window instead. The meadow outside the hotel grounds, where she had recently watched a bizarre fencing tournament, led to a wood and open country, and the road to the left brought the London-bound travelers.

She moved to the middle window and sat on the cushioned seat to gaze out and calm her silly nerves. It was a long time since any man who was not an immediate threat to her or Basil had affected her nerves. And this effect of Dornan's had never been unpleasant, simply incomprehensible.

CHAPTER TWO

H E RE-ENTERED THE room quite suddenly, a bottle and glasses clanking together as he negotiated the door. As her head jerked around, he paused.

"Don't move," he instructed and whirled into action. He all but dropped the glasses on the table, splashing wine into each, then set one glass beside her on the window seat, the other on the little desk, from which he whipped up his sketchbook and pen. He yanked up the heavy chair with one hand and set it where he wanted it before dropping into it, flipping open his book, and beginning to sketch.

"It's the way the sun is shining on your hair and your face," he said apologetically. "A sketch won't replicate the luminous texture of your skin, but I might catch enough to remind me…"

It was slightly disconcerting to have all that attention on her. His dark eyes pinned her in place as though seeing into her soul, then dropped, and rose again as soon as she began to breathe.

A smile flickered across his lips. "You needn't look so frightened. Have a taste of the wine. I'm told it's quite good."

"You told me not to move," she pointed out. "And I am not remotely frightened, merely unused to holding one position for so long."

"A whole half-minute," he said with sympathy she knew was false, and, indeed, when he raised his eyes, a beguiling laugh hung behind the focus.

"You are making fun of me, Mr. Dornan," she said, picking up her glass.

"What is sauce for the goose…"

She sipped her wine. "And what is that supposed to mean?"

"That you frequently make fun of me, so it is only civil of you to allow a little retaliation occasionally."

To her surprise, a faint heat rose into her face. "You did not appear to notice."

"As an artist, I tend to notice everything about the people or the scenes I want to paint."

"Come, Mr. Dornan. You had no desire whatever to paint me before today, and we spent several weeks in each other's company at Christmas."

He smiled faintly, but said only, "I was glad to hear that whatever danger you faced then no longer hangs over you."

She paused, the glass halfway to her lips once more. "Johnny told you that?"

"With no details, of course. But then, I never asked for any."

"As I said, you had no interest, Mr. Dornan. What changed for you today?"

"Courage, perhaps. Inspired by artistic vision, of course."

"Now you are mocking yourself."

"You deserve a rest."

Surprised laughter broke from her and his pencil, held between those long, capable fingers, flew over the page, while his steady gaze rose and fell continuously.

He changed the subject. "Why come all the way to Renwick's Hotel for a card party?"

She shrugged. "It suited my plans."

"Will you tell me what they are?"

"Would you believe, avoiding family?"

"God, yes," he said with fervor, which was interesting. "Was that your only aim?"

"No. I was helping a friend who had a great idea but lacked

the means to carry it through."

"What sort of idea?"

She considered. "I don't think I can tell you that or my reputation for discretion would fall apart. But you will be glad to know it worked and was fun besides."

He worked in silence for a few moments. "Why do you feel the need to avoid your family?"

"They are Basil's family. He stayed with them in France during my troubles that you referred to at Christmas. I fetched him away—we may have omitted to say goodbye—and now they want him back."

"Do they have a right?"

She shrugged. "In law. He is heir to the estate they live off."

"But you don't trust them?"

"I trust them to feed Basil, educate him, and look to his safety. I don't trust them to love him."

"Why not?" he asked.

"Because they won't have me living there with him."

He paused long enough to reach for his wine glass, take a drink, and set it back down on the table. "That is unkind. How old is he?"

"Eight. There is no need to tell me English boys are often sent away to school younger than that. It does not make it right."

"No," Dornan agreed. "It doesn't. But aren't you just putting off the fight by coming to Renwick's? If they traveled to England, they are unlikely to give up and go tamely back to France just because you are not at home for a day or so."

"No, but I don't have to make it easy for them, do I?"

Ne nodded thoughtfully, continuing to work.

After a while, she said, "Why do you avoid your family?"

"I don't like them. The feeling is mutual, so to be fair, there is not much avoiding to be done these days. Do you like the wine?"

"It is light and pleasing, quite appropriate for a decadent afternoon's quaffing."

His eyebrows lifted. "You find the proceedings decadent?"

"Not so far. To be honest, Mr. Dornan, I find you something of an enigma."

"How so?"

"A puritanical man who spends so much time with such cordial beauties as I met you with today, that he is quite at home with them. But then, I suppose you would have to be puritanical to withstand temptation and get any work done."

He was examining the sketches on his pad with some concentration, but now his dark gaze lifted slowly to her face, and her heart gave a funny little flip.

"Whatever makes you imagine," he said, "that I am puritanical?"

The air rushed from her lungs, for indeed there was nothing remotely pure about the heat in his eyes. And for once in her life, she could think of nothing to say.

As if nothing had passed between them, his gaze returned to his sketch, and the pencil was again busy. She didn't know how long passed before he set down the sketchbook and picked up his glass, taking a sizeable drink, though the glass still remained almost half full.

"When does Basil stop his lessons?"

"When Mr. Flowers feels he has done enough."

"Shall I fetch him?"

On the strength of that heated look, she had half-expected an attempt at seduction. Her every nerve seemed to tingle. But his question appeared to be genuine, leaving her even more confused.

"If Mr. Flowers will release him. But, perhaps I should—"

"No, allow me. Where are they?"

Chivalry, she thought with amusement, while she told him the location of their room. He was reducing the risk of her being seen leaving or entering his room. And then, he was gone, leaving her utterly bemused. Though one rather charming thought gradually emerged from her tumult.

He was not indifferent to her.

Unable to be still, she jumped up and again began pacing the room. With anyone else, including her husbands and Johnny Winter, whom she had come very close to loving, she had always known exactly what to do about mutual attraction. With Stephen Dornan, she had no idea, for either he had hidden it before or it was very sudden. Or for some reason, he was pretending.

Passing the chair he had just vacated, she paused and picked up his open sketchbook. Her eyes widened, for there was not just one sketch. Both facing pages were covered in her head in various sizes and details, in beams of light and occasionally in shadow when she had moved. One even showed her wine glass. All captured her different expressions, and she wasn't quite sure she liked that. He saw exactly when she was teasing him or provoking him, when she was amused, or interested, or even anxious as when she had told him about the Monteignes and Basil...

He worked at extraordinary speed, to have done all of those.

She replaced the book on his chair and prowled around the room once more. She would not allow this situation to get away from her. Dornan was unusual, fascinating for a man, but she was merely passing the time. Basil was her prime concern.

IN THE PASSAGE, Stephen paused, his back to the wall, his eyes closed. He'd had to leave to recover his focus. Letting her see his desire had been deliberate, to catch her expression in response. But it was his body, not his pencil, which had reacted the most, for in that instant he had seen behind her surprise to a longing, a passion that had acted on his ardor like tinder. Deliberately or otherwise, she had turned the tables.

But dear God, Aline Hagerin would be the most amazing lover... If she ever stopped laughing at him for long enough.

Pushing himself off the wall, he made himself stroll along the passage and upstairs, nodding amiably at fellow guests he met on the way. When he knocked on the door of the room Aline described, it was opened by the large tutor, who looked surprised to see him.

"I bear a message from the princess, who would like her son to join her when his lessons are finished."

The tutor looked unimpressed. "Would she?"

"May I go now, sir?" came Basil's eager voice, just ahead of his equally eager little person, which tried to catapult out of the door.

The tutor's hand descended on the boy's shoulder, pinning him to the floor. "Coat," he said mildly.

Basil spun around, trotted back to the little desk set up in what appeared to be his bedchamber, and yanked his coat off the back of the chair. "Is Mama outside in the gardens?"

"No, she's waiting to take tea with you in my studio. I'll show you." Stephen turned to go as the tutor followed the boy out and locked the door. "You will join us for tea?" he added politely as the tutor somehow inserted himself between Stephen and Basil as they walked along the passage.

"Not unless the princess requires. But I'll escort Basil none-theless."

Stephen regarded the tutor's large hand, hanging at his side. It curled into a fist. The man moved easily, without any of the slowness of many big men.

"You look like a useful man in a fight," Stephen observed.

"I've had to be with a name like Flowers."

Stephen laughed, and for an instant, the tutor's lips quirked in response. When they reached Stephen's "studio," Mr. Flowers entered very close to Basil and stood in the doorway for a moment before walking in the rest of the way.

Basil went immediately to his mother, boasting about his Latin declensions and the new wonders of mathematics he had grasped.

"I'll order tea," Stephen murmured. "Mr. Flowers, will you join us?"

"I will," the big man replied. "Thank you."

Stephen inclined his head and departed, but he was not fooled. He knew why Flowers had changed his mind—because his employer was taking tea in a man's bedchamber and it was hardly proper. The man protected the princess as well as her son. With a twinge of jealousy, Stephen wondered if there was more to their relationship.

The suspicion unraveled during tea, which might have been a tense affair without Basil, at least in the beginning. But while the boy ate cake and his mother drank tea, and Mr. Flowers provided a unique form of chaperonage, Stephen recovered his focus and quickly lost himself in trying to capture the relationship of mother and son in drawings. The nature of the woman was further revealed, not just by her clear love of the boy, but by his regard for her. Beyond the tie of mother and son, they *liked* each other, teased and laughed together.

Artistic excitement overtook Stephen's baser urges, while his tea remained untouched and his pencil flew across the pages. Only when he realized Flowers was peering over his shoulder did he snap the book shut.

"I don't care to be overlooked," he said shortly. "If it's good enough, you'll see the finished article."

"You have talent," the tutor allowed. He sounded surprised. Straightening, he regarded the princess. "Shall I take Basil, madam?"

"No, enjoy some leisure time, Mr. Flowers. We will entertain each other." But she had risen, too, and Stephen knew his time with her was over for the day. While the tutor departed, she turned her gaze on Stephen.

"So, what happens next, with regard to the portraits?"

"Painting them. Would you object to joining me in the rose garden at first light? Weather permitting, of course."

"Not at all. After this morning, it will feel like a lazy start to the day."

"Am I allowed to ask what happened this morning?"

"I'm sure it will be all about town by now. Lord Darblay and his friends held a hilarious fencing tournament at dawn in the meadow just over there." She pointed out of the window. "It caused a lot of interest—and disappointment for those who had expected a duel."

"Maida does not appear to be short of excitement," he observed.

"It does not.

"I missed the fencing," Basil said, scowling. Then he smiled. "But Mr. Flowers is going to teach me. Can you fence, Mr. Dornan?"

"I've dabbled now and again, but I'm no master of the art." A curious panic surged upward as the princess led her son inexorably toward the door. He would see her again tomorrow morning, and yet… "Would you dine with me this evening, Princess?"

The words had fallen from his mouth without permission. He was probably more surprised than the princess, who merely turned toward him with one brow raised. Not condemning but considering.

"I mean in the dining room, of course," he added swiftly. "But naturally, I understand if you do not care to dine in public."

"It has never bothered me in the slightest," she said, apparently amused. "Thank you, Mr. Dornan, I will be happy to join you. Shall we say seven of the clock?"

He inclined his head. "Until seven."

She swept out of the room. When he had closed the door behind them, he leaned on it. His mild obsession with her was blending dangerously with the bond he often felt with his sitters as he got to know them. And in this case, the bond was growing too tight, too quickly.

But more than anything, he wanted to paint her. And he wanted those paintings to be the best he had ever done. Not just for his own pride, but to do her justice.

Pushing himself off the door, he began moving the furniture that would be in his way. Then he rummaged in his trunk for the dust sheets he used to protect the floors of other people's houses when he took commissions, and spread them over the whole area from the double window, almost to the door. He set up his easels and canvases, fetched paints and pallets, and set up a small canvas for practice. He was humming to himself by the time he mixed his paints.

TO BE DINING with Mr. Dornan felt curiously like stepping into a scene of unknown danger. Which she had done on many occasions.

As she played a spirited game of jackstraws with Basil, part of her rejoiced in Dornan's invitation, in the fact that he was finally seeing her and the possibilities that could arise.

Another part, that which had kept her alive through too many hair-raising adventures, was sounding alarms and warnings because she knew in her heart, he would disappoint her. He might have challenged her view of him as puritanical, almost chaste, but she was in danger of wanting too much from him.

By the time she left Basil to change for dinner, she had resolved simply to enjoy the evening. Her heart, after all, had always taken care of itself.

In the passage, a faint, curiously familiar scent, caused her to pause and turn. Slight as it was, it drew her, searching for the root of its memory. She followed it to the staff staircase. Opening the doors, she found the smell grew a little stronger. It drifted down from upstairs.

The memory jolted into place. A similar bare staircase in Paris, an unknown, never seen man, whom she had betrayed.

She whisked herself away, letting the doors fall back behind her as she swept along the passage to her own rooms. She shoved aside the guilt she had learned to live with. It had been many years ago, after all, and the unmistakable smell of oil paints and turpentine came not from a rickety Paris tenement, but the comfortable hotel room of Stephen Dornan on the edges of London.

She had not brought a huge variety of evening gowns with her, so the choice was hardly taxing. She refused to spend too much effort on her toilette, for she was no young girl seeking to impress her chevalier. Still, Burton, her maid, announced her approval, and so did Basil when she swept back along the passage to say goodnight to him before dinner.

"I'll look in on you on my way back," she promised as she left him with the nursemaid, Ellen. She walked unhurriedly downstairs to the dining room, aware her heart was beating too fast for the occasion. Looking neither to right nor left, she crossed the foyer. From the sofa nearest the dining room, a male figure arose, and her heart turned over.

In evening dress, Stephen Dornan was stunning. She had known that, of course, from their stay at Dearham Abbey at Christmas. But now she noticed smaller, endearing qualities, like the speck of paint on his wrist and the unruly curl of hair to the left of his temple. His melting dark eyes focused on her entirely as he advanced, and, defeating her utterly, he smiled, deluging her with sunshine.

CHAPTER THREE

S IR OLIPHANT DORNAN was swaggering across the grand foyer
toward his youngest son, his elder two on either side of him
when a dazzling woman swept past them from the direction of
the staircase.

Stephen, of course, being a perfect little gentleman, rose and
bowed, though he was well beneath the notice of such a
diamond. However, shockingly, the diamond stopped and gave
the boy her hand. He smiled at her, placing her hand on his arm.

Sir Oliphant stopped in his tracks, throwing out both hands to
force his sons to a halt, too. Before their eyes, Stephen and the
beauty walked together into the dining room.

"Good Lord, has little Stephen made a conquest?" Clive, Sir
Oliphant's eldest, said in amusement.

"She'd eat him whole for breakfast," Gordon, the younger,
said contemptuously. "For some reason, she's taken pity on him."

"You're missing the point," Sir Oliphant growled, tugging
their arms to haul them back the way they had come. As one,
they retreated to the group of chairs near the front door and sat
down in a huddle.

Sir Oliphant glared from one large, handsome son to the
other. "I know he's not a normal Dornan, but he *is* a man. And
hardly as used to female attention as you two. Would *you* give up
a woman like that to immure yourself in the country?"

"God, no," Clive said fervently.

"Then is Stephen likely to abandon the chance?"

They regarded him with consternation.

Gordon said, "We'll beat him into it."

"Oh, for God's sake!" Sir Oliphant scowled. "You are not children anymore. Neither is he, despite his namby-pamby hobbies. You won't get his cooperation by *beating* him. You can't even frighten him anymore, judging by the last time we all met."

"What, then?" Gordon asked sulkily.

"Well," Sir Oliphant mused, "he's not going to walk away from her, is he? So, she must be induced to walk away from him."

Clive snorted. "That shouldn't be difficult. She'll be off after dinner."

"You always underestimate your brother," Sir Oliphant observed, although he had been guilty of that same mistake. "She is the one who needs to be scared away."

>>>><<<<

DINING WITH STEPHEN Dornan took her some time to get used to. Being the focus of such intense attention, without the relief of his sketch pad and pencil, almost overwhelmed her. Her heart fluttered continuously, as though trying to play with the butterflies in her stomach. She had never in her life felt so unsure, so...*unanchored*.

Only gradually, exchanging impersonal remarks about the food and the decoration of the dining room, did she begin to relax, recalling other residences, other dining rooms in her considerable travels. By the end of the fish course, they were exchanging amusing stories, and she was almost growing used to seeing him smile, even laugh.

Not that he was one of life's chatterers. He had talked more while sketching her, which she guessed now had been to make *her* talk. That had been to do with his art, his profession. This was different. And she liked it even more. To have his entire attention was…intoxicating.

It was also a voyage of discovery. The man she had imagined living his life in quiet artistry in England, never journeying further afield than Scotland, turned out to be exceedingly well-traveled. He knew many of the same places as she in France, Spain, Italy, and central Europe. They had heard the same musicians in different cities at different times and admired the same art and architecture.

"You were studying your art?" she said once.

"Always."

"What did your family think of that?" she asked curiously. "Because you are a gentleman, are you not?"

"What makes you think so?"

"You move too easily among the aristocracy to be anything else."

He didn't deny it. "And gentlemen do not follow such girlish hobbies as painting," he said sardonically. "Or any profession that is not the army, the church, the diplomatic service, or, at a pinch, the law."

"Which you did not consider. Then did your family not support you? How did you live? Off the sale of your paintings?"

"Sometimes. I also inherited some land in Sussex through my mother, which supports me adequately and is, besides, a pleasant place to call home." He leaned across the table to refill her wine glass. "What of you, madam? Where is your family?"

"Apart from Basil, in a better place."

He regarded her. "Your natural reticence?" he wondered. "Or am I rudely inquisitive?"

"Which do you think?"

"I think you have grown so used to keeping secrets that you have forgotten how to trust."

Devastatingly shrewd. "You wish to know my origins? My father owned a farm in the north of Spain, close to the French border. I married a landowner on the French side of that border.

Basil's father."

"What happened to him?"

"War happened to him, mostly."

"And to you?"

"I discovered I supported my own people in their struggle to throw off the French yoke." She swirled the wine in her glass and glanced up to meet his gaze. "I have a talent for dissembling."

If she had hoped to shock him, she was again disappointed. He merely nodded. "I know."

She blinked, then laughed with genuine amusement. "Apparently less of a talent than I thought."

"I am observant," he said apologetically.

"I thought I was, too. But there is a great deal more to you than meets the eye, is there not, Mr. Dornan?"

His dark eyebrows flew up. "Oh, no. I'm an open sort of fellow. A bit dull and single-minded."

"Single-minded, perhaps," she allowed.

The waiter interrupted to clear their dishes away and bring dessert—an extravagant creation of wafer-thin sugared pastry, raspberries, and vanilla cream. Although it was delicious, Mr. Dornan did not eat his, merely sat back and watched her, the faintest smile playing around his lips.

Disconcerted, she concentrated on the bliss of the sweet before her, and when she looked again, he had his damned sketchbook out, his pencil busy about the page.

"What the devil is there to draw in a woman eating?" she demanded.

"Pure, sensual pleasure."

And she, who had been trying to shock him for most of their short acquaintance, was the one who found herself blushing. The words *pure, sensual pleasure* were like a jolt of lightning in her veins, because he had said them, because he sat opposite her with his busy, graceful fingers, and she could not help but wonder about the very impure, sensual pleasures those clever hands could create.

Her entire body still tingled even after the sketchbook vanished, even as they drank coffee and spoke of unthreatening things. It came to her with another, lesser jolt, that he was an interesting man, alternately comfortable and challenging. And that, combined with the background buzz of physical attraction, was fascinating. She felt more alive than she had in years.

"More coffee?" he asked. "Or shall I order another bottle of wine?"

She regarded him, heat curling deep in her belly. His expression was polite, but his soft, brown eyes could melt a lady's bones. She could swear desire simmered there in the darkness, just waiting for her to say the word. And once, she might have.

She set her napkin on the table. "Thank you, but no. I promised to look in on Basil, and if you must begin painting so fiendishly early, I shall need my beauty sleep." Was she making too many excuses? Babbling?

If so, he didn't appear to notice, merely stood and held her chair for her to rise. She took his arm and they left the dining room, crossing the foyer to the stairs. Conversation had dried up once more. The silence was charged, yet not unpleasantly so, which was curious. There was a great deal of the curious about Stephen Dornan.

They walked along the passage, and she stopped outside the door of her rooms. "Thank you for a wonderful dinner and a delightful evening, Mr. Dornan. I shall wish you goodnight and see you bleary-eyed in the rose garden at first light."

"These are your rooms?" he asked in surprise. "I thought you would be at the end of the corridor, with Basil."

"I came to hold a card party. I couldn't have him disturbed by the noise, could I?"

Mr. Dornan's lips curved. "Of course, you could not."

She offered him her hand, though she had meant not to, just to keep the parting light. He took it and bowed, though to her surprise, he raised her hand to his lips in the European style and kissed her fingers. The touch of his mouth was light yet thrilled every nerve in her body.

"Good night, Princess. Sleep well."

Her hand was free, and he strode back toward the staircase. Blinking, she took the key from her reticule with her tingling hand and opened the door. And walked into carnage.

Dornan had already walked away, but from old habit, she closed the door to prevent anyone from seeing. Only when it vanished into a sea of calm, accepting despair, did she recognize her main emotion of the evening had been a strange, unjustified hope.

But here it was again, the intrusion of her old life, some part of it at least. It seemed that would never be over.

"Burton?" she called to her maid. If whoever had done this had hurt Burton... She could not even think of Basil yet or she would go to pieces. The rooms were silent, but she had to know what she faced before she sought her son.

Going through the motions, she turned up the lamp and replaced the key in her reticule. At the same time, she took out a slim, efficient little dagger, more than half-hidden in her hand. Picking up the lamp, she took stock as she moved through the sitting room, stepping over a fallen chair, books and clothing, and packs of cards pulled from drawers. The doorway to her bedchamber beyond was strewn with clothing, hairbrushes, and even pins glistening among it. But she could feel or smell no other presence, not even Burton's. She could hear no breathing other than her own.

Still, she kicked the clothes away from the doorway and shoved the door hard with her elbow. No one cried out or slid down the wall. The bedchamber was empty.

Nevertheless, she checked beneath the bed and inside the wardrobe before drawing the curtains and leaving in a swirl of skirts. Since the corridors were always dimly lit from the occasional wall sconce, she abandoned the lamp in her own room. But she held the little dagger firmly behind her reticule as she swept down the passage to Basil's room.

That it was locked was some comfort. She knocked once, and the door was opened almost at once by Ellen. Here, everything was tidy and normal.

"Good evening, madam," Ellen said. "He's in his bed, but not asleep. I think he was waiting for you."

Aline slid the dagger subtly back into her reticule and breathed again. She was able to smile quite genuinely at her son as she hugged him and kissed him good night. For whoever was responsible for ransacking her rooms had been attacking *her*, not Basil.

"Shall I send Miss Burton to you, madam?" the nursemaid asked.

"No, that won't be necessary. You may tell her I won't need her until morning. Good night, Ellen."

With the worst of her fear relieved, there was nothing to do but return to her own rooms and start clearing up.

"YOU LOOK TIRED."

Not the words one most wants to hear from the man who thrills one with a single look.

"What am I to say to that?" she retorted. "I could not sleep for thinking of you?"

In the early morning light, he had already set up two easels and a little trestle table covered in paints, brushes, palettes, and small bottles. He wore not a smock but a larger shirt that hung over a pair of old breeches. He looked clean and fresh, though, endearingly, he seemed to have forgotten to comb his hair, which was a trifle unruly and flopped forward over his forehead.

"I would be flattered if you did," he replied mildly, "but only if you meant it. Would you sit here?"

He picked up a folding chair that had been propped against a massive rose bush, unfolded it, and placed it for her on the grass.

She sat since it was what she had come for. Then he touched her, adjusting the position of her head, and her breath caught.

His lips quirked. "Sorry. Bad habit."

"Don't apologize, I have never been stage scenery before."

He let that one pass, more concerned, no doubt, with reproducing the colors of the sunrise, which she could no longer see.

His hands worked differently with the paintbrush than with the pencil, first in the quick mixing of his paints and then in broad, sweeping strokes that fascinated her as much as his gliding pencil work. He worked on both easels. Then he seized another brush, more colors, more delicate strokes. She lost track, simply enjoyed watching his hands, and then, more daringly, his face.

"They will bring coffee soon," he observed. "Unless you would prefer tea."

"Coffee would be welcome," she allowed. "When may I join Basil for breakfast?"

"When would you like to?"

"Before nine."

"The gardens open to the public then, and the light will have changed, so by all means. Are you cold?"

"What would you do if I was?" she asked curiously.

"Find you a blanket. I should have brought one."

"Would that not interfere with your composition?"

"Not at this stage...ah, coffee. No, don't move, I'll bring it to you."

Since he didn't seem to mind her raising the cup to and from her lips, she drank while she watched him and thought. She lost track of time until he said suddenly, "What has happened to upset you?"

She blinked. "Nothing. I am not at my best in the morning."

He snatched up another brush, made two small dabs with it, then threw it back. "If you need help, I am at your disposal."

"Why should you imagine I need help?"

"You are...not balanced."

"Is that not polite English for mad?"

He smiled faintly. "Unbalanced. It can be. You are not mad. You are wary."

"I am always wary."

"Warier," he amended.

"Not at all. I am thinking over my arrangements at the hotel and if Basil and I are to stay for another few days, we shall change rooms." It would be easier to protect Basil that way, and if whoever had ransacked her rooms last night still lingered, they would find out her connection to Basil anyway. If they didn't know it already.

Mr. Dornan scowled at the easel in front of him, then more direly at the other easel, and threw down his brush. "I can work on these more inside. May I escort you back to the hotel?"

"No," she replied, amused rather than offended by his suddenness. "But I can help you carry all this—" she waved a hand around his paraphernalia—"back inside."

"Thank you, but that would hardly be suitable."

"Well, we could walk back together empty-handed and send one of my lazy footmen to fetch it all in."

He gave in. "Can you manage the bag of paints and brushes?"

"Of course. And your canvases—"

"No," he said at once. "I shall take these." He was already throwing small dustsheets over each and stacking the easels together cleverly so that nothing touched the paintings. He could even carry them in one hand, the folded table in the other. "The chair belongs to the gardens, so we can just leave it here."

The only people around were the gardens staff—a few gardeners, who nodded as they passed, and the girl setting up her outdoor tea shop. With some surprise, Aline realized that she felt peaceful again.

It's him. He of the sculpted profile, the gentle expression, and the sharp, sharp eyes. Seductive eyes, too, when he chose...

"May I steal you again this afternoon?" he asked.

"Inside or out?"

"Out, weather willing. I'll take you for an ice."

"We should wait for Basil."

"We'll take Basil later, as well. Then you can have two ices."

She laughed. "Very well." She left him at the door of his own rooms and then went down to enjoy breakfast with Basil.

CHAPTER FOUR

SIR OLIPHANT DORNAN, sauntering along the passage, was delighted to see two footmen and a lady's maid hauling baggage out of Princess Hagerin's rooms. He tried not to smirk as he passed them and went on his way downstairs to join his sons for breakfast.

"It worked," he said gleefully, sitting down with them at their table by the window. "Her servants are wheeling out her luggage as we speak."

"As long as her people don't trace it back to us," Clive said. "Upsetting princesses—"

"Don't be a bigger gudgeon than you can help," advised his proud papa. "She's only the widow of some central European princeling, not a real princess with any power, and she's foreign. Still," he added thoughtfully, "I have to say Stephen has surprised me. Extremely beautiful woman. Wouldn't have thought she'd look twice at our boy."

"Maybe she thinks he's got money," Gordon said, receiving his breakfast with ferocious satisfaction. "After all, he apparently socializes with dukes and countesses, too. English ones."

"They probably want their portrait painted," Clive sneered. "He'll sleep with the servants."

Sir Oliphant snorted. Although he was perfectly happy to make fun of his errant youngest, he did not care for the idea of a

Dornan being treated as a lackey. It was an insult to the whole family.

"The sooner we get him home the better," he muttered, tucking into his own substantial meal. "And not just because this hotel is costing me an arm and a leg. We'll make a call on your brother after breakfast."

His sons were uncharacteristically silent until Sir Oliphant looked up and followed their gazes out the window to the terrace. The princess, the same woman who had been moving out of her rooms not ten minutes ago, was walking in the direction of the pleasure garden, laughing with a boy of about eight or nine who danced around her. She wore a pelisse of deep turquoise with a matching hat, both in the first stare of fashion. And she was in no obvious hurry. No carriage waited to be loaded with her baggage.

"I think that call on our little brother might be premature," Clive remarked. "It doesn't look to me as if she's going any-where."

Sir Oliphant swore. "So much for indirect methods. I'll give the boy one chance, and that will be all."

STEPHEN KNEW SOMETHING was wrong in the princess's world. He wasn't surprised she didn't tell him her problem, though he hadn't expected that lack of trust to bother him quite as much as whatever difficulty she faced.

Plus, he was not happy with the portraits he had begun. The sunrise and the roses were an excellent background, and the early light reflecting on her hair and skin he could make work very well. But her face was wrong. Her distracted expression, her mood, were not inspiring. At the moment, the paintings had little hope of being anything other than ordinary, decent portraits. And they should be more. He needed them to be more.

Abandoning them, he got out another canvas instead and put the finishing touches to his portrait of the Duke and Duchess of Dearham. Looking at it made him smile, which was the effect the pair had on most people. No one loved life like Johnny Dearham unless it was his Kitty. He would give them the portrait when they returned from their wedding journey, and hope they liked it.

Leaving it to dry, he set about cleaning his brushes and setting up fresh canvases. His stomach had begun to rumble by the time the knock sounded on his door. Hoping it was the princess, he was already opening the door before he realized he was still in his painting shirt. But then, she had seen him so improperly dressed this morning.

It was not the princess who stood there but one of the hotel servants, who bowed and presented him with a visiting card from a silver tray. Frowning, Stephen picked it up.

It was his father's.

His frown deepened to a scowl. No good ever came from his parent's communications. And what the devil was he doing here? How had he even known to find Stephen here?

He turned the card over to find a message in his father's distinctive scrawl.

Join me for tea at four.

A father certainly had the right to command his son, and the son had a duty to obey. But Stephen knew of old the dangers of complying with Sir Oliphant's orders too precipitously. And he had besides, more or less promised to accompany the princess and Basil for ices.

"Is there a reply, sir?" the servant asked respectfully.

"No... That is, yes, there is—one moment." He walked over the dust sheet to the desk and without sitting, seized a piece of the hotel paper and dipped the supplied pen nib in ink.

Without troubling with a greeting, he wrote, *Unfortunately, I have another appointment at four. I shall be free between six and seven and if convenient, shall call upon you then. Stephen.*

Folding the note, he wrote his father's name on the outside

and returned to the servant. "In which room is Sir Oliphant staying?" he asked, dropping the note on the silver tray.

The servant told him and went on his way, leaving Stephen thoughtful and not a little suspicious. He could think of no reason for his father to seek him out. Even a bereavement could have been conveyed by letter.

He removed the paint-splashed shirt and cleaned himself up before changing into more respectable garb, and went in search of the princess. Which, since he knew she was changing rooms, was unexpectedly difficult. The hotel staff were unlikely to tell him which rooms *she* occupied, and he didn't want to risk talk by asking. He had just decided to ask staff to send a message begging her company when he saw the distant but unmistakable bulk of Mr. Flowers entering a door on his right.

Speeding up until he came to the same door, he knocked. A youngish maid opened it, and Basil's voice could be heard shouting, "Mr. Dornan!"

The maid opened the door wider to reveal a large sitting room, off which led three other doors. On one side, a desk had been set up, presumably for Basil who was leaping away from it with joy.

"Forgive the intrusion," Stephen said, entering. "Good afternoon, Basil! Flowers. I was looking for the princess."

"I'm here." Dressed in a becoming shade of turquoise, she emerged from a door at the far end, presumably her bedchamber. "Come, we shall leave the scholars to their studies. Basil, be good and there might be ices later. Thank you, Mr. Flowers."

The casual thanks was given with a quick, direct smile, and Stephen thought the tutor and all her other staff would be her willing slaves just for such genuine appreciation.

She seemed also to be genuinely pleased to see Stephen.

"Your new rooms are satisfactory?" he asked as they left the hotel and walked toward the path to the pleasure gardens.

"Much better, I think. Basil has the other bedchamber and my maid and the nursery maid share the small room. Mr. Flowers has the room next door. I can hear music!"

"It will be the end of the midday concert," Stephen said. "We can go and listen if you like."

They caught only the last ten minutes, though in that time, he made several sketches of her rapt face, and even one of the wry glances she cast at him once she realized what he was doing.

Afterward, they strolled to the canopied tearoom, and Stephen devoured a bowl of rich broth with fresh, warm bread. After which, he got out his sketchbook and drew her eating flavored ices.

"Better than Gunter's?" he asked.

"Do you know, I think it is!"

When she had finished, they walked around the garden, finding interesting little corners and hideaways.

He said, "I would like to paint you in the moonlight, on one of the public ball nights when the place is lit up with lanterns and torches."

"Will there not be too many people peering over your shoulder and barging between us?"

"That's why I'm looking for a place that will be lit but not occupied. What is up here?"

A few steps through overhanging bushes led to what looked like a secret little garden with a lily pond and elegant fronds. A little waterfall poured into the pond and a stream led away down the slope.

"I wonder if this is the place Kitty told me about?" the princess mused. "It is rather beautiful."

"And there are lanterns hung above."

"We could bring our own, too, if you needed extra light."

"True. I could imagine you here." At the moment at least, it was a place of peace and warmth and solitude. And being alone with her here, so close he could inhale her perfume and feel her warmth brushing against him, was both tempting and intoxicating.

"I can imagine you here, too, with your easels set up…here."

She pointed to the grass by the pond.

"And here, perhaps." He leaned against a boulder, partly to ease the tension caused by her nearness, and regarded her. He could not help smiling. "From any angle, you are so beautiful, I doubt my ability to do you justice."

People—men—must say things like that to her all the time. And yet a hint of color stained her delicate cheekbones as she gave him an amused, skeptical look. "You are an artist. You should be able to see that I am not. My features are not quite regular, my nose too long, and my mouth too wide. And I have it on the best authority that my chin is too determined for femininity."

"Beauty is not that kind of symmetry or perfection," he said impatiently. "Whoever told you it was is a nincompoop."

She laughed at the word, and he smiled all over again at her spontaneity. "Come, shall we explore further?"

By the time they returned to the hotel, there was still an hour left of Basil's lesson time.

"Would you let me paint you for that hour?" he asked.

Her gaze was direct. It always was. "Where?"

"In my studio."

A smile flickered across her face. But to him, this was the true description. He happened to sleep in the room that was his temporary studio. He didn't think of it as painting in his bed-chamber.

"Why not?" she said lightly, leading the way upstairs. As he followed, he allowed himself a quick glance around the public areas for any sign of his father. In fact, he kept his eyes peeled, until they were inside his room when he closed the door behind them with some relief.

"Where do you want me?" she asked with a trace of the old, teasing provocativeness he had seen so little of today.

Inevitably his body answered silently, but with his voice, he was able to say easily, "In the window seat again, if you would."

Her fingers hovered over the buttons of her pelisse. "Do you want me to leave it on?"

"I want you to be comfortable."

As she removed the pelisse, he took off his own coat and threw it on the bed before snatching his painting shirt from the top of the trunk. His breath caught at the picture she presented, like ice in the sunshine, waiting to melt. The warmth in her eyes contrasted achingly with the calmness of her face and the cool, turquoise fabric of her gown.

He began to paint at once, both entranced and determined, inspired and desperate. He knew instinctively that this one would be good. She took form on his canvas in the tones of her skin and hair and the almost exact color of her gown. He would work on its shades of fold and shadow later. For now, he needed its boldness, her expression, and her beauty to shine through...

"My rooms were ransacked last night."

The announcement came out of nowhere and took a moment to penetrate his paint-obsessed brain. His brush stilled. He frowned. "Ransacked?"

"Ransacked. I found it like that when I returned from dinner with you."

"Dear God, why didn't you tell me?"

She was silent, and it came to him that she didn't know. She was too used to dealing with problems—dangerous problems, he more than suspected—alone.

"Did you even tell your servants? Flowers?"

She shook her head. "I need good, loyal servants. I don't want them taking fright and running."

"If they do so, they are hardly good or loyal. Their job is to protect you and your son."

"I know, and I believe they would. But first, I need to know who did it and why."

"Have you any ideas?"

"Three," she said. "The first that it was a total stranger, who just happened to get into my room and wanted to make a mess. It wasn't a thief, though, for nothing was taken. My opinion is that while possible, this idea is unlikely to be the case."

"I would agree, but you should have a word with Renwick anyway. What is your second possibility?" He had begun to paint again, to catch that particular brave tilt of the head, her sheer *aloneness*.

She sighed. "The Monteignes. My first husband's family want Basil back. It would be easy enough for them to have discovered by now that I am here and to send someone to frighten me. Basil's room was untouched, which bears out this theory. I believe this to be the likeliest possibility."

"Then I think it's time the Monteignes were made aware of how many friends you have in London, more than ready to break Monteigne bones or shoot them over twenty paces."

A smile flickered once more. "Why, Mr. Dornan, I had not realized you were so bloodthirsty."

"I can be on occasions," he replied, restraining his anger because it would not help her. Or the painting. "What is your third theory?"

"Ah. Well, that is harder to articulate. It could have been someone who was once my enemy and has not forgiven me. You are aware, I suspect, that I have often been in...odd situations where I have acted to bring information to the right quarters. Or feed lies. I have done...bad things for what are, to me, good reasons, but not everyone will see it like that."

His heart swelled with pride in her courage. He understood fully why Johnny Dearham had once been so obsessed with her. Her strength was awe-inspiring.

He drew his brush back and focused all his attention on the flesh-and-blood woman. It wasn't difficult. "I think you have someone particular in mind."

"Not really." She shifted uncomfortably. "Smelling your paint just reminded me of a mistake I once made. In Paris, during the Hundred Days before Waterloo. There was an established chain for passing information. I knew none of these people, never met them. But I carried several messages to an attic by the Seine. I climbed the stairs with the scent of oil paint and turpentine in my nostrils and slid pieces of paper beneath a door. One day, I knew I was being followed, knew it was time to go. But first, I took my followers on a tour and lost them to make one last delivery to that attic. I decided it was worth the risk. And it was, for me. But when I looked back, men were swarming up the stairs. I had led them there."

Stephen stared blankly in shock. She was reliving the experience, and he...

He swallowed. "You could not have known. Better that he was caught than you, and in any case, you don't know that he was arrested, or anything else." He paused. "Or do you?"

She shook her head. "No. And as I say, that man is only one possibility who might consider I betrayed him. There are other more obvious enemies."

"Would they really waste their time on revenge, four years after Waterloo?"

"Probably not," she agreed. "I only mention it because it has been on my mind recently. My own money is on the Monteignes."

"And that is why your son's tutor is also a talented pugilist?"

"And I keep two almost as large footmen in the room next door," she admitted. She refocused her gaze on him. "I wanted you to know, though I'm not sure why."

"I'm honored that you told me," he said truthfully. And touched, and moved beyond words by her trust.

"Is it time to fetch Basil?" she asked restlessly.

WHEN THE WORDS had burst free, she had been as surprised as Mr. Dornan. She had only been mulling over what his reaction might be if she told him what had happened. And suddenly the story spilled out. And not only that, but the Paris fiasco that she hadn't even thought of for years before coming to Renwick's.

As they fetched Basil and hailed him off for an ice, she still didn't know what had prompted her to tell, unless it was the strange, growing closeness of artist and sitter, a closeness cemented by their time in the gardens this afternoon. By the lily pond, he had stood so close to her that she had wanted to rest her head against his shoulder, slip her arm around his waist. She still wondered what he would have done. Would he have jumped free in shock? Or turned and kissed her?

She didn't think the shock terribly likely. Seeing him in the company of Lord Calton over Christmas, comparing him to the younger, more rakish version of Johnny, had given her a probably false impression of him. He could not look as he did and be a stranger to women's pursuit. But he took it in his stride, from the waitress's fluttering eyelashes to her own teasing. He might not be rakishly indiscriminate—she suspected he was not and rather liked the fact. His kisses, his love, would be *worth* something.

Where the devil had that thought come from?

Blinking, she refocused on Basil, whose eyes were sparkling in delight as a bowl of ices was brought to him. But he waited patiently while she poured the tea and passed a cup to Mr. Dornan.

He cast her a quick smile. He sat in a quite unorthodox position, leaning back in his chair with one knee propped against the table edge and his sketchbook balanced there while he drew. His focus shifted from her to Basil and back, as though he were making sketches of each, or perhaps of their interactions.

She had never imagined the relationship between a portraitist and a sitter could be this...intimate. And yet it felt oddly comfortable. Even Basil, who had grown wary recently, of new people—probably since she had left him in France with the Monteignes—seemed accepting of Dornan's restful company.

And then, "Ah," said an amused male voice. "Now I understand why you were too busy to keep an appointment with your old papa."

A tall, thin gentleman of middle years had appeared behind Mr. Dornan. Beneath the sagging jowls and the lines and shadows of premature aging, he possessed similar features, though there was something wrong about the eyes.

Stephen Dornan's pencil stilled, and for a moment, he did not raise his eyes from the page. Then, without turning he said, "I merely postponed it for a couple of hours. How are you, Father?"

Two younger, bigger men had materialized at either side of Mr. Dornan senior.

"In the pink," one of them said, reaching over Stephen's shoulder to pick up his teacup and drain it.

"Thanks to us," said the other. "While you...what?" Without warning, he whipped the sketchbook from Stephen's hands. "Make children's drawings? Good God, little Stephen, do people actually pay you for this tripe?"

The spite in his mockery shocked Aline. This was not mere brotherly raillery. This was...bullying, confirmed by the sneering laughter of the other brother and the complacent smile of the father.

Stephen did not react in any obvious way. He did not try to snatch back the book or even curl his fingers in rage.

Instead, he said mildly, "Manners, gentlemen." And pushed out his chair so suddenly that the brother with the book was forced to leap backward. "Madam, allow me to present Sir Oliphant Dornan, my father, and my brothers, Mr. Clive Dornan and Mr. Gordon Dornan. Father, Princess Hagerin."

Aline did not offer her hand, but at least the men moved away from Stephen to approach her side of the table and bow.

"My son," she said distantly, while every nerve prickled in alarm to have such men so close to Basil.

"How kind of your highness to allow my boy to practice his drawing around you," the father said indulgently.

"And, bless you, he needs the practice," Clive said with scornful amusement. He tossed the book to Gordon who laughed and pushed it onto the table in front of Basil.

"*You* could make a much better job of drawing your mama, couldn't you, my boy? Go on, try. And when you're grown up, you can call out my talentless brother for the insult to your beautiful lady mother."

Basil, bless him, closed the book and passed it to Aline, though his color had risen and he had that mulish, glittering look about him that had once preceded a tantrum. Clive, meanwhile, had returned to Stephen's end of the table and now seized him with an arm around his throat while he scrubbed his knuckles brutally hard against his brother's head.

"Pleased to see us, little brother?" he chortled. "Of course you are!"

To Aline's distress and fury, Clive began to haul Stephen by the neck out of his chair, attracting attention from the other patrons and the waiting staff. "Come on, time to give the lady some peace. The little prince there will be a better escort fo—"

Before Aline could move to intervene—as she most surely meant to—Stephen's chair somehow shoved hard into Clive's middle. The arm at Stephen's throat loosed, and with a sudden twist and clatter of movement, suddenly it was Clive who sat in the chair, blinking, an expression of ludicrous surprise on his face.

While Sir Oliphant and Gordon stared at Clive in astonishment, Aline quietly rose and, with Basil, walked around the other end of the table.

"I believe it turns insalubrious in the garden," she drawled. "Your escort, Mr. Dornan?"

Stephen, whose wary gaze was divided between his family and the two burly waiters approaching from the kitchen area, turned at once, offering her his arm.

CHAPTER FIVE

A S THE THREE of them walked away without a backward
glance, Aline passed Stephen Dornan his sketchbook, which
he slipped into his pocket.

He said quietly, "I apologize, madam. My family's clowning is
tedious at the best of times. Before a lady and her son, it is
unforgivable."

"They weren't clowning," Aline said shortly. "They were
belittling you in front of me. Or trying to."

"I didn't like them," Basil pronounced, peering back over his
shoulder. "I'm glad I don't have brothers."

"Not all brothers are as annoying as mine," Stephen said.

"They're placating the waiters," Basil reported.

"Well, they won't want to be thrown off the premises," Stephen said. "At least, not yet."

"Did you know they were here?" Aline asked.

"I knew my father was at the hotel. I received a note com-
manding me to tea."

"Then this was punishment for not obeying?" she asked in-
credulously.

"No," Stephen said thoughtfully. "That was a deliberate scene."

"They seem an entirely different *species* to you."

A flicker of a weary smile crossed his face. "In that, they

would agree with you. Now you know why I avoid family. But at least the ices were good."

"Better than Gunter's!" Basil enthused. "The raspberry one was delicious, but I think the chocolate might be my favorite."

"Mine, too," Aline agreed, and for the rest of the walk back to the hotel, they discussed ices and jugglers and other fun things about the gardens. Stephen joined in, making ridiculous suggestions about other entertainments that could be introduced, including elephants to spray the guests in summer to keep them cool, and lions and tigers to chase the stilt people.

Basil laughed, and even Aline was smiling as they walked along the passage to her new rooms. A footman admitted them to her knock, and Basil began to explain to him and Ellen about the elephants.

Apparently assured of her safety, Stephen Dornan bowed, clearly about to take his leave.

"A moment," Aline said quickly. "You do not mean to keep the appointment you made with your father?"

"I am a dutiful son," he said sardonically.

"Are you?"

"No. But I am as polite as I can be. And besides, I need to know what they want before I can say no and be rid of them."

"Be careful," she said austerely. "Better still, I shall accompany you and use my august presence to prevent violence."

The surprise in his eyes melted her heart. "That is the kindest of offers, but I must decline. For one thing, I would not subject you to them twice in one day. For another, I have been dealing with them all my life and know how to manage them."

He hadn't fought for the sketchbook, knowing his brothers would merely toss it between them until it was damaged, forcing them to find another way to torment him with it. He had broken Clive's hold and escaped him without violence or temper. Perhaps he did know, but she could not like it.

"Then have dinner with me afterward," she blurted. "Otherwise, I shall worry."

His eyes warmed. "Will you? I could not have that on my conscience, too. On the other hand, it would not be a pleasant meal if my family joined us in the dining room."

"Then we shall dine here," she said recklessly. "Mr. Flowers can join us as chaperone."

He was silent, perhaps recognizing that Mr. Flowers, as well as the footmen, were excellent guards. But his eyes were focused unblinkingly on her face. "They won't actually hurt me, you know. They are family, and they need me to do something. But I shall gladly dine with you and Mr. Flowers."

With that, he bowed and walked away.

"REMIND ME," SIR Oliphant said coldly to his elder sons when they were once more ensconced in his rooms, "not to listen to any of your ideas ever again."

"Why not?" Gordon demanded, almost hurt. "She didn't care for the scene, and we made him look pretty small."

"And yet she walked off on his arm, leaving us to be told off by the damned waiters!" Sir Oliphant snarled. "No more public scenes."

"Whatever you say, Papa," Clive muttered, flexing his shoulder.

Stephen must have twisted it for him when he'd flung the bigger man in the chair. Although it went against his own interests, Sir Oliphant was fiercely glad someone had punished the fool.

"So, what do we do now?" Gordon demanded.

"Talk to him like a human being," Sir Oliphant said, somewhat reluctantly conceding that the days of bullying Stephen might be over. "Tell him what we want, and I'm sure he'll agree to come home with us."

"And if he doesn't?" Clive asked skeptically. He stretched out on the sofa with his feet up on the cushions. He hadn't troubled to remove his boots.

Sir Oliphant bared his teeth. "Then we'll favor the direct approach and be done."

His sons speculated on that directness with obvious pleasure, until a knock sounded on the door.

"Prompt," Sir Oliphant observed, encouraged, and jerked his head at the door.

Gordon rose from the chair he'd been lounging in and opened the door. "Stephen," he said with mock affection. "Look, Papa, Stephen has honored us with a visit."

"I have," Stephen agreed, walking in and leaving Gordon to close the door behind him. "But I can't stay long. I have a dinner engagement."

"The beautiful princess?" Sir Oliphant said before Stephen's brothers could mock. "Quite a catch you have there. I'll be honest—never thought you had it in you."

"I don't. We merely have an agreement that I paint her portrait."

"Whatever you say, Stephen. Budge up there, Clive, let your brother sit down."

Reluctantly, Clive moved his feet and sat up to leave space. As though he didn't notice, Stephen sat in the armchair.

"So why have you followed me here?" Stephen asked. "What is it you want?"

"Do we have to want anything?" Sir Oliphant tried to sound hurt, though he probably wasn't very good at it, for Stephen didn't even think about his answer.

"Yes. You have no stomach for my company, nor I for yours, so let us get to the point."

He had never used to sound so damned sure of himself. He used to at least *try* for filial respect and civility. But then, Sir Oliphant hadn't seen his youngest for...three years. Five if one ignored the mere bow they had exchanged in Bond Street in the spring of 1816. Well, Stephen had bowed. His father had stared, for Stephen had been in the company of some very fashionable and clearly wealthy young men who were quite unknown to Sir Oliphant.

"The point is," Sir Oliphant said slowly, taking the other armchair and leaving the space on the sofa for Gordon, "that we want you to come home."

Not the faintest smile crossed Stephen's face. "Run the estate into the ground, have you?"

Jesus. The boy had always been this annoying, but did he have to be quite so blunt? "It's not doing as well as it might," Sir Oliphant said with some dignity. "Not nearly as well as it did before you departed."

"Departed," Stephen repeated without emphasis.

It was true Sir Oliphant had thrown him out because he wouldn't leave the damned painting alone, had refused to study for the church or join the military. The word was, he'd gone abroad, despite the war. "Well, we needn't quarrel over the past. I have to admit you were good with the land, with the demesne, and the tenancies. And your own place at Kennings looks to be thriving. So, we would like you to come home and work a little of your magic."

Still giving nothing away, Stephen moved his gaze to his brothers. "You all want this?"

The boys nodded emphatically, so like chastened schoolboys that even Stephen's lip twitched.

"Hire a steward," he said mildly and rose to his feet.

Time, then, for direct action. Sir Oliphant didn't budge, but Clive and Gordon sprang up and stood between their little brother and the door.

"Really?" Stephen sounded amused. "Then don't hire a steward. It's nothing to me. But if you want me to think about my answer, you'll sit down."

They shuffled out of the way, and Stephen strolled to the door. "I've thought. Sort out your own damned mess," he said and walked out.

STEPHEN COULDN'T DENY it felt good. Perhaps it was petty of him, but he had been bullied too long by his brothers while his father stood back laughing to have any time for any of them. And although he had overcome his anger against them for the most part, his parting words felt like closing the door on the past, on the family who never wanted him, and whom he no longer needed.

He really was free, his own man, and had, besides, a growing success in his art. He had made his way in the world, professionally and personally, without any help from them. And that was the way he liked it.

As he returned to his room, he shook off the encounter, leaving only the mild euphoria of victory, and looked forward to his evening with the princess. He washed and changed into evening dress, dragged a brush through his hair, and set off for her rooms. He encountered a few fellow guests on the way, heading down to the dining room, but recognized none of them.

Only as he turned the corner to the princess's rooms did a warning frisson run down his spine. He was being watched... Or the princess's rooms were. Remembering what had happened to her old rooms last night, he kept walking, straight past her door, flexing his fists, but even as he turned to face whatever danger lurked behind, someone rushed toward him, and something dark and smelly blinded him. A sack had been flung over his head.

Holding him strongly from behind, someone tried to yank him off his feet. Someone else was actually *lifting* his feet. Not so much an attack as an abduction. But he could not afford to be abducted. The princess had to be warned of her danger, protected at all costs. Fear for her lent strength to his instinctive, sudden struggles.

He kicked out hard with both feet and connected with grunting flesh. At the same time, he crashed his elbow backward and freed himself from his other captor.

"The bag!" someone hissed as Stephen reached for the odiferous covering over his head. And then, someone, probably the man who'd had him by the feet, leapt upon him from behind, yanking the bag downward. Stephen heaved with all his might, and his attacker went flying over his shoulder, crashing, by the sound of things, into his fellow.

Stephen snatched the bag from his head, blinking in the sudden light, just in time to see the edges of two large men staggering around the corner. They seemed to be dragging each other, so either they were desperate not to be seen, or he'd managed to injure one or more of them quite badly. Ferociously, he hoped the latter.

He longed to chase after them, but first, he needed to see that the princess was unharmed. He strode up to her door and rapped once before clenching his hand and drawing it back to punch.

Mr. Flowers blinked at him. "Something I said?"

Stephen lowered his fist with a shaky breath of laughter and walked in. Through the open door to one of the bedchambers, Basil's voice could be heard arguing, presumably with his nurse. A maid was fussing with a table that had been set up near the window. And alone on the sofa, sat the princess, paying him no attention. She was staring at a piece of paper held in her hands.

Stephen went straight to her, sinking onto the sofa beside her. "What is it?" he demanded. "What has happened?"

"Nothing," she said, crumpling the paper in her hand and trying to smile.

He covered her hand with his. "Don't."

Her gaze flew to his, and held, and then, almost to her surprise, she opened her hand and let him take the crumpled note from her.

"Someone slipped it under the door," she said. "Just a few minutes ago. I thought it was you, saying you could not come after all."

He spread the note out. The words were few and printed in

easy-to-read letters.

GO HOME. THINK OF THE LITTLE PRINCE.

Something went click in Stephen's memory, and stretched rapidly, wretchedly into understanding.

"They are threatening Basil," she said in a low, shaking voice. "This changes everything..."

Flowers had appeared beside them and Stephen, still going over the evidence in his mind, wordlessly passed him the note.

"We're all thinking of the little prince," Flowers said savagely.

"No, we're not," Stephen said. Both the princess and the tutor turned stares of outrage upon him. "Basil is not a prince, is he? He is the son of your first marriage."

Panic, clearly, had stopped her thinking, but she thought now. "Some people would not know that."

"Some people clearly do not," Stephen agreed. "But Basil's family *do*. Enemies you might have made during the war would surely know. All your London acquaintances know. If anyone had troubled to follow you here, they would surely be aware that Basil is not a prince."

The princess searched his eyes. "You think you know," she accused.

"I do," he said ruefully, "though part of me wishes I did not." He dragged his fingers through his hair, drawing her attention to his slightly rumpled appearance, the tear in his cravat, an irritation on his face thanks to the disgusting sack.

"Stephen Dornan, have you been *fighting*? Was that the noise I heard? I thought the staff had dropped something in the corridor..."

"Sort of." He drew a deep breath. "First, I believe you and Basil are both safe. This note, and what happened last night, I believe to be the work of my family."

"Your *family*?" she exclaimed while Flowers scowled, completely baffled.

Stephen sighed. "This was all aimed at me. My father and my

brothers want me to go home and sort out the mess they've made of the estate. They clearly thought I wouldn't be able to tear myself away from you, and so they've been trying to persuade *you* to leave *me*."

"By frightening me," she said slowly. "And then by belittling you, and finally, by threatening Basil."

"Clive called him a little prince this afternoon," Stephen reminded her, "and they have no idea that he isn't. They don't move in your circles. When they come up to London, it's for sport, gaming, drinking, and wenching. And they don't like that I won't do as they want."

"Then you were wrong. They will hurt you! They *did*."

Stephen smiled. "I think all my panicked thrashing around hurt them considerably more. Don't worry. If they're still here tomorrow, I'll put them right on a few points, including the breadth of your influence and your protection."

The princess appeared to be speechless.

Flowers said, "You had better be right about this."

"I know."

Aline rose to her feet and walked to the decanter on the side table. "I think we all need a glass of sherry." Her hand shook very slightly as she poured it out, but her voice was steady.

Stephen's admiration grew. He wanted to put his arm around her and hold her in comfort. He wanted to throw his father and brothers out the window. Any window, as long as it was high up.

"I'm sorry," he offered as he accepted a glass from her.

"I believe I am relieved." She gave the other glass to Mr. Flowers. "Although I'm sure we would both like to know how you came off best against two much larger brothers."

Stephen thought about it, though not for long, for he was very aware of her seated beside him, even at a distance. "I've grown bigger and fitter, and they have got fatter and slower. Although as I said, the panic helped." He raised his glass, "To you, Princess, and Basil."

Flowers raised his glass in return, and they all drank rather

51

thoughtfully. When her footmen came in with trays of food, the princess's mood seemed to change to one of gaiety. It was, probably, a social trick, but it lifted the mood and set the conversation flowing until the good cheer was genuine.

It was an amusing evening, mixing banter with intelligent conversation. Mr. Flowers proved to be a highly interesting man, a scholar, and a pugilist, though how far he took either activity remained a mystery.

The footmen served the meal from covered silver dishes, replenished glasses, and removed each course when it was done. Basil came to join them for dessert and was then sent reluctantly off to bed. The princess led her guests back to the sofa and offered them brandy or port. The footmen were given leave to retire, once the remains of the meal were cleared away.

Stephen, basking in the princess's vital presence, could have stayed there all night. But after one glass, Flowers clapped him on the shoulder. One knew when Flowers was attracting one's attention. "Come, then. Time we wished the princess good night and left her in peace."

Stephen did not mistake him. He was acting correctly and making sure Stephen did, too. It wasn't just the boy he guarded. Stephen allowed himself to be drawn from his seat, added his thanks for the delicious meal and the delightful evening, and followed Flowers to the door, where they both bowed. Flowers walked along the passage toward the next door.

Stephen turned for a last glance at the princess. Candlelight glinted off her hair and the translucent skin of one side of her face. The other side was in shadow, making it mysterious but no less alluring. Like two sides of her many-facetted character. But the image stayed him, striking him like a blow.

"Princess, would you consider letting me paint you now?"

CHAPTER SIX

"**H**ERE?" SHE ASKED dubiously.

"It would make a lot of noise moving everything. My studio is already set up."

She hesitated, but only briefly. "I have my key, Burton," she said to the maid. "Open the door to no one."

"Of course not, madam," the maid said, as though shocked.

And so, they walked the distance from her rooms to his, almost like a couple going home at the end of a pleasant evening. He liked the thought of that. Imagined them going home together every evening—and pulled himself up for a stern, if silent, talking to.

Inside his room, he turned up the lamp and turned his attention to the unlit fire in the grate, for the room was cool at this time of the evening. Besides, the flames provided the kind of glowing light he wanted.

When he rose and turned, he found her watching him. "Where do you want me?" she asked, with more genuine humor than the first time she had said the words to provoke him.

"On the bed."

This time it was her eyes that widened in shock, a hundred expressions chasing each other across her face, too quickly to read. He liked to think there was a flare of desire in there, but he also knew wishful thinking when he came upon it.

"If you are not offended," he said. "I would like to paint you sitting on the side of the bed, here."

Following his gesture, she brushed past him, allowing him to inhale her distinctive scent, and sat where he asked. "People will speculate that I granted you too many liberties."

"As part of the set, I believe it will be understood as the pose it is to those who know you. But we don't have to show it. I would like to try it, but you will always have the final say as to whether or not it is shown or even kept."

"Do your worst, Mr. Dornan," she said lightly.

"That is not much encouragement to an artist." He took off his coat, threw it over the chair, and pulled on his painting shirt.

"I don't think you need encouragement."

He pulled a few easels around him, changing the distance and angle of his view with each. He settled on the middle one, from where he could see her in detail between the bedposts, though he secured canvases to each, just in case the notion came upon him.

Inspired, he strode over to her, raising his hands to position her as he wanted her. Her veiled gaze followed his every move.

He paused. "Permit me?"

Her nod was infinitesimal. Very gently, he touched her cheek, turning her face toward his favored easel. Her skin was so soft he wanted to linger, to know her by touch rather than mere sight. She did not jump when he took hold of her red, lace-trimmed shawl, loosening it so that it fell around her elbows as though she were shrugging it off. Thus, the beauty of her shoulders and chest was also revealed, down to the fashionably low-cut neck of her evening gown.

She was so lovely, she caught at his breath. Slowly, so that he didn't startle her, he touched her hair, seeking and finding the correct pin. A lock of hair freed itself and tumbled to her shoulder where it nestled, drawing attention to her creamy skin. The effect was a fine, sweet line between sleepy and decadent. It was an effort to keep his focus on art, on painting rather than devouring the pliant woman on his bed.

She trusts me.

The words echoed in both wonder and warning. He stood back and moved to his easel, from where he couldn't help smiling. "Perfect. Thank you."

As a last-minute courtesy, he poured the remains of yesterday's bottle of wine into two glasses and placed one for her on the bedside cabinet before returning to his easel and lighting more candles behind him. He took a thoughtful drink of wine, surveying the somehow moving figure on the bed, forcing himself to consider technicalities of light and shade, color and brushstrokes.

And then he was mixing paint, desperate to capture her as she was now.

"Did you love him?" he asked, not so much because he wanted to know as because he wanted to bring the softness of sensuality to her face. Yet having asked it, and won something of the expression he sought, he hung upon the answer.

"Johnny? Yes, a little. Not that I ever told him so, but I had never met anyone like him before, so grasping of life and all its pleasures, and yet determined to do the right thing by his innocent sister and her friends. And by traitors."

"That is a story I don't know."

"I suppose it is not mine to tell. But one day I expect he will tell you."

"Did you come back to England for him?"

"No, I came to remind the British government of its obligations. When the prince died…" She hesitated, a wealth of sadness passing through her eyes, drooping the corners of her soft, suddenly vulnerable mouth. "I played a rare, bad card. In the midst of danger, I pretended to be with child, thinking it would preserve my position and my wealth. But the new ruler wanted no rivals, and I had to flee."

She reached out and took a delicate sip of wine. "Although I will further confess that when I saw him—Johnny—again, I did think it might be fun to marry him. After all, he was a duke now and even more intriguing than he had been as a younger man. But then there was Kitty. I never meant to like her."

"You stepped aside."

She let out a breath of cynical laughter. "I never had the chance. Without trying, she stepped right through me."

"Do you mind?"

"No." Again, the smile playing on her lips was a little sad, though not heart-breakingly so. "Neither he nor I were the same people, and it had only ever been a fling. I like to see him and Kitty together. It brings me hope."

"Hope? Of what?"

The smile grew deprecating. "Of the one true love every girl secretly dreams of. You are wicked, Stephen Dornan. You have caused me to betray a foolishness that does not sit well with my character."

"Not with your invented character, perhaps. Would you call me Stephen?"

"To distinguish you from your brothers?"

"No, just to hear my name on your lips."

Her eyes grew luminous. Dear God, how could he paint when she looked at him so?

"Are you flirting with me, Stephen?" she drawled.

"Did you think I could not?"

"I thought perhaps you *would* not. But you haven't answered my question."

It seemed he was still painting after all. "I don't know the answer. Is it flirting to tell the truth?"

"I think it depends how you tell it."

He smiled. "You have an answer for everything."

"I wish I did," she said ruefully.

He left it in the air while he worked, but when she said no more, he prompted, "Such as what?"

"Such as... Were my actions during the war with France truly as right as I thought at the time? Even enemies of one's country—and one's adopted country—have good reasons for what they do."

"Including you," he pointed out.

She took another sip of wine, and set down the glass, pushing it impatiently away from her. "And the person who lived at the top of the stairs that smelled of oil paint and turpentine. I had no reason for that. Was my information worth his imprisonment? His torture? His life?"

He paused and stared at her helplessly. He drew in a breath, "Aline—"

"Ignore me. I grow maudlin. It must be the wine and the smell of your paints that reminds me of the past. Tell me instead about *your* life and loves, Stephen Dornan."

"I paint portraits," he replied. "And like you, I am still waiting for my one true love."

"Waiting, not looking?"

He knew what she was asking, and it was most improper. But she had already trusted him with her feelings for Johnny Dearham.

"I am not a monk."

"But you keep no mistress in Kensington or in Mayfair. At least not at the moment."

He smiled at his painting. "How do you know that?"

"I asked Lord Calton."

"Why?" he asked baffled.

"Because you always intrigued me."

His heart skipped a rapid beat, disconcerting him. Or perhaps she had done that. He darkened the shadow among the painted folds of her shawl, added a touch of orange to the glow from the fire striking her hair, but he was in no condition now to paint. The intimacy had overtaken the task.

He laid down his brush and stepped back. "You always daz-zled me," he said conversationally.

She made no reply, and he was afraid to look. Instead, he turned the easel so that the canvas faced the wall. He hadn't touched the others.

"I have reached a good place to stop, and you must have a crick in your neck." He pulled the paint-strewn shirt over his head. "Allow me to escort you back to your rooms."

"Are you afraid your brothers will attack me?"

"No. But I will take every second of your company I can."

She eased off the bed in slow motion, as graceful as it was arousing. She walked toward him, the shawl still dangling from her elbows. "While throwing me out of your room," she mocked.

He swallowed. "While trying to keep you safe."

"From you, Stephen Dornan?"

He could no longer tell if she was mocking him. Her beauty, his own body, both clamored too much. "Yes." He had to move away, blowing out all the candles, and turning down the lamp by the door.

He turned to find her right beside him. His heart seemed to be knocking against his ribs. But fear of losing her trust, her friendship, was drowning in the possibility that there could be more. That he wanted, needed more. Beyond that, he could not think, only feel.

"I would like," he said, gazing down into her warm, brilliant eyes, "if you would allow it, to kiss you good night."

Mutely, she lifted her face to his.

SHE HAD BEEN on the verge of taking matters into her own hands. The strange, unbearable intimacy of the last hour—or more, she had no concept left of passing time—had done its work too well. Just feeling his gaze upon her had aroused her unbearably. Combined with the constantly growing surges of affection and trust and fascination, she found it near impossible not to touch him.

And now he touched her first, lifting one slow, paint-stained hand to glide his fingertips across her cheek. She closed her eyes, and his hand settled, cupping her face as his breath kissed her mouth.

And then came his lips with the tiniest of touches on hers, followed by a brushing caress as light as a butterfly wing. And a small soft kiss at the corner of her mouth, another that moved gently to capture her parted lips at last, tasting, savoring.

Her hands crept over his shirt, to his shoulders, his nape, as she sighed with wonder as well as pleasure. No one had ever kissed her quite like this before. It felt like awe, like worship, and she never wanted it to end, for it was sweet and enchanting. She didn't even realize she wanted more until he gave it, sinking his mouth deeper and moving on hers with slow sensuality.

With a sigh, she opened wide to him, winding her tongue around his, and drew him closer, her fingers tangling with the soft hair at his nape, her other arm around his waist, her palm flat against the astonishing heat of his back. She pressed nearer, discovering with fierce triumph that he was already fully aroused. He made no effort to hide it from her either, even moved his hips languidly against her as he kissed. God help her, he would be a uniquely sensitive lover, giving pleasure after pleasure.

His free arm swept around her, holding her fast for a long, delicious moment. And then his mouth loosened, smiling against hers. "You kiss as you look."

"What does that mean?"

"If I ever find out, I'll tell you."

"I hope, at least, it is good." She hoped she didn't sound as defenseless as she felt.

"You have no idea." He pressed his lips to hers once more and then stepped back, reaching for his coat.

Had she ever been this unsure before? He would not even ask her to stay, and she could not suggest it for fear that her kiss had not inspired him *enough*. He was not like the other men she had known. He had discernment and she...she was no innocent. She had married twice for sentiments that had never quite reached the height of love. Or at least, she didn't think they had.

He deserved, better, purer... But devil take the man, no one had proposed marriage.

He shrugged into his coat, and, either ignoring or forgetting his cravat, offered her his arm and opened the door.

"Am I required tomorrow?" she asked lightly.

"At sunrise, in the rose garden, if you are not too tired? I'll wait for you."

Will you? "Very well."

"Aline?"

"Stephen?"

There was a pause. "You take my breath. All of it."

She had no idea what to say to that, so she remained silent, letting the warmth and gladness seep through her. From the stairs, she could hear voices below, and a door closed above, but they reached her rooms without meeting anyone.

He raised her hand to her lips, not a chaste salute to her fingertips, but an open-mouthed kiss on her knuckles. "Until the morning. Sleep well."

And then her hand was free, and he strode back toward the stairs.

SIR OLIPHANT WOKE to darkness. Despite the fuzzy head caused by last night's brandy, he had the unpleasantly clear feeling he was not alone. He turned over in the comfortable bed and peered into the darkness. Surely a blacker darkness formed the shape of a man at the foot of his bed?

"Clive, is that you?" Sir Oliphant growled. "Go back to bed, for God's sake. I'll listen to your apologies tomorrow, and they had better be abject."

"You should have taught them better when they were young," said a freezing voice, one who should have sounded as familiar as Clive's but did not. "I never saw why I should be the only one to be caned."

"You squealed more," his father sneered before he remembered he needed this son on his side, although it appeared now to be a lost cause.

"I imagine everyone squeals at five. Or was it four? No matter. I came to discuss the future, not the past. In particular, the future that will be yours and my brothers', should you ever threaten Princess Hagerin again. Or even *hint* at a threat. Did you imagine she was some hapless refugee relic of a minor foreign princeling no one has ever heard of? That she has no friends in this country? Allow me to disabuse you.

"Among her friends, she counts the Prince Regent and Lord Liverpool. Also, the Duke of Wellington, the Duke and Duchess of Dearham, the Marquess of Sedgewick, and the entire Gorse clan. Several earls and government ministers are not only her friends but exceedingly protective. Accordingly, were they to hear of your mean, disgusting behavior to her, you would find yourself blackballed from every club in London—and most hells, besides. You would be cut in the street. And no one, *no one* would ever lend you any more money. Am I making myself clear?"

"No," Sir Oliphant snapped, refusing to give in although his stomach was roiling in dismay. "I have no idea what you are talking about."

"No? Shall I discuss the little prince? Who is not, by the way. Shall I visit my brothers and see how many bruises have formed on their faces and bodies? I do have an unmannerly urge to rub this sack in their faces." As he spoke, he threw it at his father's head. "Although on the whole, I can't really be bothered. So, I will tell you this once, and once only, before I inform His Grace of Dearham of your nasty tricks. You and my brothers will leave here before ten this morning, and you will go home. When I hear you are there, I will send you a steward at my own expense. If you do not allow him to do his job, then you may sink into perdition with my utter indifference."

He rose and moved sure-footed toward the door as though he

could see in the dark. Perhaps he could. Perhaps that was why, even with a sack over his head, he had defeated both his larger, more manly brothers.

The door handle rattled. "If we are ever obliged to meet again, a mere nod will do. For once in your life, Father, make the right decision."

Cool air whispered into the room and then the door clicked shut.

CHAPTER SEVEN

A LINE MADE HER way to the rose garden at sunrise the following morning with butterflies in her stomach and her heart both eager and afraid of meeting him again. No one kissed like Stephen Dornan. No one moved her like Stephen Dornan. She had no idea where it was leading and that both frightened and excited her.

Though she had sprung out of bed, washed and dressed for the occasion with such enthusiasm that she would be well served if Stephen himself slept through their appointment. Would he have painted more last night, working on the same portrait of her that had absorbed him the evening before? Somehow that absorption, that intense focus on her had aroused a slow, blistering desire.

She saw at once that he had set up his easels and canvases in the same place as yesterday. His sketchbook lay precariously on the edge of his paint table. But of the man himself, there was no sign. She moved toward the easels, wondering where her chair was. Perhaps he had gone to fetch one. She took a moment to admire the beauty of the sunrise. Although she didn't think it quite as spectacular as yesterday's, she gazed with new appreciation at its pinks and golds.

Inevitable, the easels were covered. She gazed, tempted, at the sketchbook. If she were just to pick it up and see where it opened, surely that would not be spying on unfinished work? In truth, she didn't want to spy on how he saw her. In fact, she thought she was rather afraid of that. She just wanted to look at his work, as though through studying it, she could learn more of the man.

Still, seeing no sign of his approach, she stooped and picked up the sketchbook. Holding the spine in one hand, she let it flop open. The pages revealed to her were around the middle of the book, some time before they had met at Maida. And yet, the full-page faces looking back at her were *her*. One with a teasing smile, the other contemplative, almost sad. Almost exactly as she had felt when she realized she no longer wanted Johnny Dearham. And wanting nobody had made her sad.

Wanting nobody and yet noticing everything about Stephen Dornan. She closed the book and replaced it on his table before wandering around the empty, scented garden. And then she saw him in his painting clothes, snipping roses from their stems at apparent random. Over his arm, he carried a shawl.

He glanced over and lifted his hand before striding over to meet her. "Good morning! I went over to ask Bill Renwick if I could cut some of these roses because yesterday's painting wasn't quite working. I wondered if you would hold these, and pretend to pick some more? It would provide context for your presence. And we can still use yesterday's sunrise."

So, straight to business. "Where do you want me?" This time, the words spilled out without intent, and to her surprise, she actually blushed.

But he paused, his gaze flying to hers as he handed over the shawl to protect her arm from the thorn. He didn't blink. "Anywhere," he said softly. "God help me."

Her blush deepened, flooding her entire body.

But as if he hadn't spoken, he pointed to the tall rose bushes behind her. "Can you reach up for one of those roses while holding the others? I'm afraid your arm will tire, but we'll do it in spells. Tell me when it hurts. Glance back at me over your shoulder…"

AT A QUARTER before ten, Sir Oliphant stepped down from the hotel toward his waiting coach—a ramshackle old thing that should have been replaced years ago. He all but shoved his sullen sons inside, for Gordon's face was bruised where Stephen had kicked him, and Clive sported a bandage around his head, having landed on it, apparently, when his little brother threw him on the floor.

Their pathetic blundering had led to this humiliating departure, and he was *not* in charity with either of them. Neither, of course, was he in charity with his youngest, who, despite agreeing to send a steward to sort out their estate problems, had spoken to his father quite without respect, ordering him around as though he were an ill-behaved stable boy rather than a baronet.

That rankled. It rankled so much that Sir Oliphant had told the hotel clerk that Stephen would pay the shot for the entire family. A petty but necessary revenge since none of them but Stephen had the wherewithal to pay such extortionate charges. The hotel was not even in town.

Before he followed his sons into the coach, he glanced to the right, toward the pleasure gardens which were quiet at this hour, although the staff were busy. He looked the other way and glimpsed a couple arm in arm, walking along the grass at the side of the drive that led to the main road to London. They paused, the man pointing around him, perhaps to the new canal or the view of the city.

Sir Oliphant knew another surge of resentment, for the man was his son, and the woman with him was Princess Hagerin.

"Your pardon, sir," interrupted a polite voice, and Sir Oliphant turned to see a distinguished man of about his own age touching the brim of his hat. "Might I ask if you are acquainted with that lady?"

Old habits died hard, and it took an effort of will not to slander her just to spite his son. However, bearing in mind her powerful connections, he held his peace. Besides, the fellow addressing him sounded French. Sir Oliphant had never cared for the French—or for anyone really who was not English. He preferred to forget that he himself had been named for a Scotsman, as had one of his sons, thanks to a drunken promise he had apparently made to his wife.

"I have met her," Sir Oliphant replied briefly. "I am more acquainted with her companion."

"Who is...?"

This was bordering on rudeness, but the Frenchman's blatant curiosity aroused Sir Oliphant's. "My son," he replied mildly. "Mr. Dornan."

The Frenchman's eyes remained civil and friendly, but they were remarkably shrewd. "Forgive me, sir, but I think you do not approve of your son's...friendship with Madame la Princesse."

"Not for me to say," Sir Oliphant muttered. He would have turned away, but the Frenchman spoke again, this time offering his hand.

"I hope you will also forgive my vulgar curiosity. Allow me to explain. My name is Monteigne, Philippe de Monteigne. This is my son, Charles de Monteigne. My brother's son had the honor to be married to the princess."

"The child is not a prince," Sir Oliphant muttered sardonically, as he reluctantly shook the hand of his new friend. He nodded curtly to the younger man, who appeared happy enough to wait in the background.

"Not to the world, sir, but to me, he is as good as a prince. He is, in effect, the head of our family, and the heir to the land Charles and I manage for him."

"Good for him," Sir Oliphant replied, tiring of the pointless conversation. "If you will excuse—"

"Your son is, no doubt, a most estimable young man," Monteigne interrupted.

A derisive snort came from inside the coach.

"But," Monteigne continued, "my concern is for the head of my family. I cannot have her dragging the boy around Europe and keeping him from us. A boy needs his male relatives."

In other words, he wanted control of the boy to be sure of his own position when the child came of age. Sir Oliphant had no quarrel with that—or much interest in it either.

"My question, sir, is this. From your observation, is the boy safe? Well-guarded?"

Sir Oliphant, his boot already on the coach step, lowered his foot to the ground and, scenting an opportunity for mischief, led his new friend away from the people coming in and out of the hotel.

"It is interesting you mention that. The boy has a tutor built like the side of a house and there are two footmen almost as large. While I love my son, I cannot pretend he is an eligible partner for a princess, or anyone related to a distinguished family such as yours. My son is a so-called artist, a ne'er-do-well, a rake of little conscience. He was even in Europe—France itself, I hear—during the late wars, and that is not something his own people would approve of."

Sir Oliphant smiled and managed a few more barbs against his son, all but chortling over his own cleverness in getting around Stephen's conditions by slandering, not the princess, but Stephen himself. "By all means, take her and the boy out of his influence," he finished nobly. "As a caring father, I would be grateful. Good day, sir."

With that, he tipped his hat and climbed into the coach. He waited until the coach moved away before he broke into delighted laughter.

ALINE AND STEPHEN Dornan spent large parts of the day together. After the morning sitting in the rose garden, he joined her and Basil for breakfast. Basil seemed pleased with the company, chattering away about what he was learning with Mr. Flowers, the pleasure garden, ices, and the joys of toy soldiers.

Stephen didn't tease him or talk down to him in that jovial way adults tended to. Instead, he spoke to him much as he did everyone else, with serious interest, leavened by breathtaking flashes of humor that Basil shared.

"Would you look at my drawings?" Basil asked once. "Mama and Mr. Flowers say they're good, but I'm not sure Mr. Flowers knows as much about art as Latin grammar and mathematics."

"I would love to see them," Stephen said at once, but Mr. Flowers had just been admitted, and it was time for lessons. "Perhaps at lunchtime?"

Aline thought Stephen would bolt off to work on his paintings, but he suggested a walk, and she was glad to join him. The odd breathlessness she always felt around him had become a familiar, pleasurable background to their growing closeness. She had no idea where this strange relationship was going, if it would end with her portraits. But for the moment, she was happy to grasp it with both hands.

Returning from their walk in the woods—he behaved like a perfect gentleman throughout—he spoke briefly to the hotel doorman.

Rejoining her, he said, "My father and brothers have departed the hotel, leaving me to pay their shot! But at least they have gone. Tonight is the public ball in the pleasure garden."

She blinked. "Are you asking me to dance?"

"I'm asking you to pose for me at the lily pond if the light is right."

"Of course," she agreed. Taking her courage in both hands—when had dealing with a mere man become so difficult?—she added, "Shall I see you before then?"

He smiled. "As much as you like. I may not be much company, but your presence delights me."

It was fortunate, perhaps that they had to stand aside to allow two elderly ladies to pass them, for her entire body was flushing with delight of its own.

She let him work alone for an hour while she dealt with her correspondence and listened to the occasional hum of Basil and Mr. Flowers talking. Then she ordered coffee, left a cup for Mr. Flowers, and took two more upstairs to Stephen's "studio."

When she knocked, his distracted voice bade her enter. She doubted he even registered who had come in as she silently laid the coffee beside him, but a smile did flicker across his face as he worked.

She was tempted to peek at the canvas before him, for an impression at the corner of her eye caught the shape of his bed and a fold of red shawl, and she knew he was working on last night's painting. The others scattered around him were all covered.

She took her own coffee and sat in the armchair. The quiet was rare and oddly soothing, and she loved to watch him work.

His paint-stained hand reached out and grasped the dainty cup. He drank with his critical gaze still on the canvas, then unexpectedly glanced up and caught her eyes. He smiled as if seeing her there was a surprise, and her heart gave its inevitable flutter.

"Thank you for the coffee. All is well?"

"Basil is wrestling with mathematics. It brought back un-pleasant memories, so I vacated the room."

"You struggled with mathematics?"

"No, I struggled with the teacher, who was my brother's tutor, and saw no reason why a female should know such things."

"I thought the Europeans were more enlightened than the English about educating women."

"Not this European."

His gaze dropped to her lips as she spoke and grew fixed. She wondered if he wanted to kiss her again, and then he returned to the painting, so presumably he had merely spotted some flaw in his work. She drank her coffee mostly in companionable silence, with only the odd conversational overture.

Once, she asked, "What do you want me to wear for tonight's painting?"

"Something diaphanous," he replied without thinking. "If you have nothing like that with you, anything will do…" He stepped back, examining what he had done, then set down the brush, covered the canvas, and moved to the next easel.

At last, she stood, collected his empty cup and saucer, and moved toward the door.

"Aline?"

She turned back.

"May I join you for luncheon?"

Gladness flooded her. "I'm taking Basil to the pleasure garden again, but you are very welcome to join us."

"Then I shall find you there."

The threat of Stephen's unpleasant family might have gone, but Aline saw no reason to let down her guard. After all, she had come to the hotel for reasons that had nothing to do with Stephen. So, allowing Mr. Flowers his well-earned break, she summoned the footmen, who were well-versed in keeping a discreet watch on Basil's safety.

Basil brought his paintings to show Mr. Dornan, who dully sauntered toward their table, once more in gentleman's attire with only a few paint marks showing under his fingernails and a small spot of white in his hair that she itched to pick off for him.

Naturally, Basil thrust his pictures at him as soon as he had sat down. Waving aside Aline's protests with a quick smile, he examined the drawings and paintings, which Aline thought were rather good for Basil's age, though she was well aware of her own bias.

"These show definite promise," Stephen said at last. "I like your imagination and the way you use colors is particularly good. You have your own style and a good eye."

Basil beamed, and Aline could have kissed Stephen in front of everyone.

"Will you teach me more, sir?" Basil asked eagerly.

"Of course," Stephen replied without hesitation.

Which made Aline uneasy. Promises made to children, even more than any other, had to be kept. She would be very glad to have Stephen in their lives for as long as he would stay. But after his portraits of her were done, she rather suspected he would be off to immerse himself in his next commission.

After they had eaten, they walked in the gardens. Stephen bought a ball from a stall that had just opened, and he and Basil played football on the grass. Mr. Flowers joined them for a more riotous game, and eventually so did two of the stilt walkers and Dennis, the footman. Aline looked on benignly, pleased and laughing.

Before long, other boys came to join in, and the men reduced their role to watch. Stephen came and stood beside her.

"It is good for him to play with other children," she said. "I have hauled him around the world too much. He needs to settle and make friends."

Stephen nodded.

"I thought he would have that when I married the prince. But the best-laid plans... We had to flee and for his own safety, I had to leave him with the Monteignes until I could rectify matters."

"But you are settled now, are you not? In London."

She nodded. "Providing there is a way to spike the Monteignes' guns."

"There is always a way," he said vaguely.

Later, as on the previous afternoon, he painted her in his "studio," and then moved to the painting of her and Basil. He had them discuss Basil's drawings, with them spread out on the floor, while he watched with his steady, dark eyes and worked who knew what magic with his paint and his clever, delicate hands.

Leaving him to work on his own for a couple of hours, she took Basil back to their own rooms. Just as she put the key in the lock, some movement caught the corner of her eye and she spun around. No one was there.

"Did you see someone?" she asked Basil, hiding her unease.

"No. There's no one there," Basil assured her.

Perhaps her nerves were getting the better of her.

CHAPTER EIGHT

S TEPHEN DINED WITH Aline and Mr. Flowers, who then helped Stephen cart his easel and other equipment up to the lily pond. The weather remained dry, if a little cloudy, but, Stephen assured her on his return, the glow of the lanterns was spectacular, coming from all over the park, and he had not given up on a little starlight.

Aline, wearing a scarlet domino cloak borrowed from the hotel in order to blend in with the other guests no doubt swarming the pleasure gardens by now, handed a matching one to Stephen.

His eyes laughed, although he donned it without a murmur of complaint.

"You look like some evil monk from something by Mrs. Radcliffe," Aline said.

"So do you."

Basil came out and laughed at them both before allowing his mother to hug him goodnight. Then, with the servants and a scowling Mr. Flowers to see them off, they made their way out of the hotel and into the pleasure garden.

They were not the only people crossing from the hotel. Most of the others were masked and walked straight to the pavilion where the public ball took place.

"Aren't you tempted?" Aline asked as they walked on through

the colorful throngs laughing and chattering their way about the paths.

"To dance with you? Of course. But I would rather have you to myself."

The gardens were different at night, at least on a ball night. Waltz music drifted out from the pavilion. The neglected, shabby appearance of the ornamental temples and castles and fountains was hidden in the lantern light, which turned the whole place into a magical, fairytale world.

Apart from the odd feminine screech and lascivious laughter from the bushes.

They discovered their secret garden was still secret. The close reeds and bushes and a spreading willow seemed to distance them from the noise of the rest of the park, though the waltz music was still faintly audible.

While Stephen lit the extra lanterns he had brought over and positioned them to shine on his easel, Aline cast off her domino and gazed about her in wonder, from the pond to the sky where the passing clouds did indeed reveal a scattering of stars in their dark velvet firmament. In a moment of pure euphoria, she lifted her arms and spun around, smiling up at the moon.

"Do that again," Stephen said breathlessly.

Laughing, she did so. He made her repeat the twirl, and half-way through caught her to a halt. Her heart skipped, thinking he would kiss her, but he didn't, just adjusted her face to look beyond him to the sky.

"Can you hold that pose?" he asked, raising her arms as they had been before.

"I can try..."

He seemed to work furiously fast, though from her position to the side, she could not see him so well. After several minutes, he said, "Lower your arms if you like and ease your neck. I'm working on the background... The gown is beautiful, by the way, just what I envisioned."

He was working on a larger canvas than he had used for the

other paintings, though he did not look remotely daunted by the size of the task he had given himself.

"Do you ever *not* paint?" she asked curiously.

"Sometimes, when I'm just sketching. But no, not for very long."

"And yet you don't miss much of what else goes on in the world, do you?"

"I try not to. Subjects for art are everywhere. Could you hold your head up again?"

She obeyed, but apparently, it wasn't quite right, for he came toward her, and adjusted her stance and the angle of her head. Then he paused, and to her secret delight, stroked a caressing thumb across her lips.

Then he left her and continued to paint.

"Now," he said sometime later, "can you spin as you did before? I need to catch the movement of the gown... Again, if you please... And again if you're not too dizzy! Now rest a few minutes."

It was the pattern of the evening, repetitive and tiring in many ways, and yet it was never dull because she was in his company, and, especially during her resting time while he concentrated on aspects of the background, they talked about anything and everything. And laughed. When she had met him at Dearham Abbey at Christmas, she had never imagined him capable of so much laughter, or so much quiet, subtle humor.

"One more spin," he said, "and then we should go back before you freeze to death."

"I am not such a poor creature." She obliged, and he gave a soft grunt of satisfaction. Since he didn't tell her otherwise, she held the pose. Then she heard his movement to the side, the rustle of fabric, and her domino cloak landed about her shoulders.

She glanced up at him smiling and heard his breath catch. He still held her lightly by the shoulders, his fingers somehow warming through the fabric of cloak and gown. His steady gaze dipped from her eyes to her lips, causing her to look at his, which was a mistake for a spurt of longing hit her that was only part desire.

And then his lips came closer and took slow possession of hers. No kiss had ever begun with such silken softness and overcome her so completely. Stephen Dornan did not snatch and devour, but savored, persuaded. At once sensitive, and deeply, sensual, he let the passion grow and grow.

She sighed into his mouth, deepening the kiss because she could do no less, and he held her, caressing her back and the bare, sensitive skin of her nape.

"Warmer now?" he asked huskily as they come up for breath.

"Much," she whispered.

He released her slowly, and, it seemed, reluctantly, in order to gather up his paints and brushes, to cover his painting, and fold the easel for ease of carrying. She carried the bag of paints and brushes. They abandoned the lanterns and went carefully down the steps and across the garden to the main path, which was quiet now. Even the music had stopped, although a lot of noise came from the pavilion area.

"Is it midnight?" she said in surprise. "It must be the unmasking."

"Which is an excellent time for us to escape back to the hotel."

As they did so, she was aware of every inch of him and of herself. The doorman offered assistance with their burden, and Stephen rejected it with cheerful thanks. Neither Stephen nor Aline voiced the suggestion, yet she continued with him upstairs and along the empty passage to his "studio."

His bedchamber.

The door closed on the world beyond.

"Are you tired?" he asked casually, taking the bag from her and setting it down beside the easel. "Or would you mind if we continued with last night's portrait?"

He straightened and, with odd deliberation, met her gaze.

She held it, her heart drumming against her ribs. "Is that really what you want?"

A smile flickered across his lips. "No. I'm scrambling for a gentlemanly reason to ask you to stay."

"You already gave me one." Boldly, her heart quaking, she took a step nearer him. "When you kissed me."

They stared at each other. She didn't know whose breath it was she heard, labored and shallow. Expressions chased each other through his eyes, most of them strangely desperate. And then he moved, sweeping her almost off her feet and into his arms. Her stomach dived, her whole being delighted in the power of his arms, the hardness of his body, and the sudden, untamed passion of his kiss.

"I have wanted you since the first moment I saw you," he uttered into her mouth.

Her answer was lost in his kiss, and by the time that ended, she could no longer recall the question. He pressed his stubbly cheek to hers, and she tangled her trembling fingers in his hair.

"Please," he whispered in her ear, his breath unbearably arousing, "may I take you to bed?"

"If you don't, I shall be very—" The rest was buried in his mouth.

Surprisingly, it seemed, he would give in to the urgency of passion, which suited her very well. But even as she clung, dragging his shirt—both his shirts—up over his chest, he stepped back and threw them off himself and stared at her with clouded, yet glittering eyes.

"Let me undress you," he said unsteadily and held out his hand in an oddly courtly gesture. She wound her fingers around his and allowed him to lead her to the bed, where he tugged back the covers, and then slowly turned her and began to unfasten her gown.

It took a long time. She didn't mind, for his mouth teased and kissed at her nape, and she could not be still. More kisses traced along each of her shoulders as he finally let the diaphanous muslin and net gown drop down to her elbows. Unlacing her stays was accomplished quickly and deftly, and then her chemise untied as he kissed his way down her back, making her shiver and undulate.

His arms reached around her, sweeping the gown off her arms to the floor. His hands held the curve of her waist, stroking, then caressing their way upward to softly cup her breasts through the thin lawn of her drooping chemise. She closed her eyes and leaned back against him in bliss, and when his fingers circled more boldly, teasing her nipples, she reached blindly for his mouth and found it.

The chemise vanished, and his fingers played on her naked skin. She turned in his arms, running her hands greedily up and down his back, her open mouth buried in his throat as she inhaled his warm, masculine *Stephen* scent. She dragged her mouth across his clavicles and down his chest, and found herself on her back, reaching blindly for the buttons of his pantaloons.

To her surprise, he let her, even knelt over her to give her access while he gazed down at her hands, at her breasts, her face, breathing heavily. And then he scooted off her to kick off the remains of his pantaloons and drawers. As though he had just discovered them, he took hold of her ankles, then slowly caressed his way up her leg to unfasten one garter, and then the others. She had never found the removal of her stockings so slow or so thrilling before because it seemed his lips had to explore every inch of exposed skin.

"Stephen," she all but panted, grasping his hair.

His smile was voracious as he pulled himself up, covering her body with his long, lean one. She found delight in sweeping her hands up and down his length, in moving her hips against the long, hard column of his erection. There were more lingering, blissful kisses, the intimate exploration of his fingers, and then his lips, down her throat and collar bone and breasts. She loved the way he responded to her every touch, sighing, undulating, softly groaning his desire.

With growing desperation, she writhed beneath him, arching up into him. His lips, his tongue, found her breasts, leading her to desperate, panicked need. Only then did he enter her body, slowly hilting himself within.

"Oh..." she whispered. "Oh, Stephen..." She gazed deep into

his eyes, and he into hers, and then he began to move, and she with him.

His hands grazed her cheek, her lips. "How can one person be this lovely, this…"

"You are," she whispered, unable to hold back the bliss. "You are…" She reached again for his mouth, and he gave it, sweet and sensual.

It was the first of many joys she found in his arms, until, the greatest of all, when he rose up over her writhing body, withdrawing, and allowing his own magnificent passion to release at last with hers.

WHEN STEPHEN AWOKE, he was warm, deliciously happy, and tangled in Aline's gloriously naked limbs. Never had he found such intense pleasure as in making love with this woman, this unique, beautiful woman, who was everything he had ever wanted and so much more.

Where the devil did that come from? But, no, he wasn't even surprised by the knowledge. It had been creeping up on him, galloping on him since he had begun to know her here, building on the voracious desires of his body.

Which had been quite right. She was a magnificent, generous, utterly passionate lover, and her joy moved him as no other woman's ever had. Despite her experience—or perhaps because of it—there was something sweetly vulnerable about her.

Levering up on one elbow, he gazed down at her in the pale dawn light. *I adore you.*

He did, with every fiber of his being. And he loved that it was so.

He wanted her again. He also wanted to paint her thus, tangled with the sheets, beautiful in her well-loved, rumpled debauchery. He smiled at the thought. Painting her so intimately, without permission, would be a betrayal. Besides the moment was between her and him, and he was *honored* to have her in his bed. Honored and thoroughly aroused.

He shifted, just to touch her hair, the soft skin of her cheek, keeping it light so as not to wake her. Or at least give her the chance to go back to sleep. But he saw her delicious lips stretch into a smile, and when he skimmed a finger over them, they moved to kiss it. He needed no further encouragement to replace it with his mouth, teasing her to full wakefulness. The kiss deepened slowly, delightfully into one of utter sin as his body settled over hers, caressing, worshiping.

Her response was sleepy yet savoring. "I thought I had dreamed you in my bed."

"You must have. For here you are in mine."

Her eyes opened, already clouded with passion that almost undid him. Taking him by surprise, she pushed, rolling him onto his back. At least she came with him. And, perhaps in revenge for his slow approach last night, she began to caress him with her knowing fingers and her mouth, covering his body, chest and stomach and...

He closed his eyes in bliss. *Never stop that. Never leave this bed. Never leave me.*

The gift of such pleasure deserved reciprocation, which he was more than happy to provide, while the sun rose higher behind the curtains and spilled dappled light upon her beauty.

"It must be nearly nine," she murmured sleepily into his throat as they lay tangled together, sated once more. "I need to see Basil. And wear something less decadent than that evening gown."

"Smuggle yourself in with the domino cloak still around you," Stephen advised as she began to untangle herself and sit up. "I wish you could just stay here." *I wish we didn't have to pretend.* But that led in a dangerous direction, and he was relieved to be distracted by her slender, naked back.

She glanced over her shoulder at him, her eyes tempting, and yet suddenly veiled. "I could come back."

"To be painted?"

"Of course." A smile, wicked and entirely Aline flashed across her face and was gone. Hastily, she collected her strewn clothes and donned them with her back to him. It crossed his mind that even after the intimacies they had enjoyed, she was shy.

"You are so beautiful," he said softly. In new and wonderful ways that astounded him. "Shall I fasten your gown?"

"There is no point when I am about to take it off again." She found one stocking and sat on the bottom of the bed to slide it over her foot.

Stephen, spotting the other under the dressing table, rose from the bed and retrieved it. He knelt before her and took her bare foot into his hand.

"What are you doing?" she asked warily.

"Helping you to dress. After all, I was largely responsible for the undressing."

A bewildered smile flickered in her eyes and was gone. She watched him as he slipped the stocking over her foot and drew it up over her calf and knee. Her breathing changed when he reached her thigh, but she did not stop him. It was hard to stop himself and tie her garter.

She seemed embarrassed now by his nakedness, for her eyes slid away and would not meet his as she rose and swung the domino cloak around her. He did not wish to part from her so. In fact, he was aware of rising panic.

Hastily, he struggled into an old dressing gown that dangled over one of the bedposts and made it to the door, just as her hand closed around the key.

"You will come back?" he blurted.

Her gaze flew up to his and seemed to lighten. "If I can."

He bent and kissed her lips, not a lover's kiss, but a soft, brief one of affection. And then she was gone, leaving him already longing for her return.

Unless she already regretted what they had done.

CHAPTER NINE

H IS ANXIETY THAT he had done something wrong, scared her away so soon, twisted through his joy in last night and his effort not to think of the future. At least, not beyond her return to his room while Basil stayed with his tutor.

He knew only too well the beguiling intimacy that could spring up between painter and sitter. But he had never before taken advantage of it, had never wanted to. The intimacy, from his side at least, had always been platonic. Until Aline. Who was just…overwhelming. Unique. Wonderful.

He distracted himself the only way he knew. Having put the bed to rights and tidied up, he washed and dressed in his old painting clothes, and set about cleaning the brushes he had left out last night. Only then did he allow himself to look at all the portraits he had begun of her so far. He scowled at them, trying to be objective, and came to the relieved conclusion that they were all working. And as long as he didn't mess it up, the one he had begun last night in the secret garden, would be the center-piece, large and bold, full of movement and joy and life.

He set to work on it once more, filling in what he had only sketched out of the trees and bushes in the background, working backward from the bits of reflection he had already painted in the pond.

He had just begun on the unpainted stretch of sky when a

knock on the door heralded not Aline but the chambermaid with fresh water and towels. He turned down her offer to clean the room, all but shooed her out, and returned to his painting.

Which was when it hit him. Today was Sunday. There would be no lessons for Basil, no reason for her to leave him in the care of others in order to be with him. Disappointment swirled. But perhaps he could join them instead. The weather seemed pleasant enough—perhaps a country walk and luncheon al fresco?

He finished the sky and found his heartbeat quickened just by looking at his painting of her.

You are pathetic, Stephen Dornan. He covered the painting and moved to the next. And the next. Until he knew that if he was going to invite Aline and Basil to walk, it should be now. Hastily, he cleaned his brushes once more, and his hands. He was about to change when a knock sounded at the door.

Refusing to allow hope to overwhelm him, he strode to the door and opened it.

Aline breezed in with a basket. And he could only smile as if he had been given the best, most unexpected gift.

"Are we going on a picnic?" he managed.

"Picnic, yes," she replied, setting down the basket on his dressing table. "Going… Not unless you want to."

From her basket, she took two glasses and two empty plates, followed by full plates of sandwiches, pastries, cold meats and fruit, and a bottle of wine.

He began to laugh. "Aline, you are magnificent."

"Mr. Flowers is taking Basil to play football in the meadow with some of the local boys we met in the gardens yesterday. It is a boys' activity, and his mother's presence is neither required nor desired."

It was a delightfully decadent afternoon, all the more so for the feeling of it being stolen. They ate and talked and made love, and took the remains of wine to bed where, a little later, they made love again.

Emotion and knowledge settled around Stephen, too new

and precious to examine too closely. He merely enjoyed her, enjoyed the present and every pleasure it offered, large and small. And then, they washed and dressed respectably once more, packed up the basket, and left the room.

Stephen returned the basket to one of the hotel staff, and then, arm in arm, they went in search of Basil.

BASIL WAS DISCOVERED in the meadow where Aline had recently watched Lord Darblay turn a dangerous duel into a fencing tournament. She spared a thought for Darblay and Gina Wallace, whom she hoped were married by now, or at least well on the way to being so. But mostly, her mind and her heart were full of Stephen Dornan.

This morning, her emotion had frightened her. It was nothing she could control and that had never happened to her before. No one, neither of her husbands nor even Johnny Winter, had made her feel like this. And she had no idea what to do about it.

And then it had come to her. She should do what she had always done, what came naturally to her. Make the most of it.

If it didn't last, she might be relieved. If it grew...well, she didn't know how she would bear it. But she would not sit alone in her rooms wondering if he regretted her or if he would leave her now he had had his wicked way with her.

He had put her stocking on with such tender, sensual grace... He had asked her to return when she was already regretting making the offer. And so, she had rediscovered her courage and done as she wished. And dear God, she was glad. Stephen was a man of hidden depths and intense, relentless pleasures.

She had never felt as thrillingly, wonderfully close to anyone as she did to Stephen as they walked arm and arm to the meadow and found Basil saying goodbye to his new friends.

Mr. Flowers looked a trifle frazzled at the edges, but Basil and the footmen had clearly had a wonderful time.

"Mr. Flowers, my thanks," she told the tutor. "You deserve a little time to yourself, so please, consider yourself off duty until tomorrow morning,"

"We're going to play again tomorrow," Basil said. "At mid-day."

"It will be a shorter game tomorrow, then," Aline warned, but even that seemed to be fine with Basil.

At her invitation, Stephen joined them for dinner. None of the servants batted an eyelid at the indiscretion. Burton, after all, must have had a fairly good idea where Aline had spent the previous night.

And that evening, she again returned to Stephen's "studio," to let him work on the painting of her on the bed. Every nerve tingled with awareness as he adjusted the folds of her shawl and the angle of her face. And she melted completely when it seemed he couldn't help kissing her before he returned to his easel.

He was more disciplined than she. Even so, tension crackled between them. Even though she was suddenly so tired she could barely think. Perhaps he was, too, for as he cleaned his brushes, he said, "Will you stay? I shan't pester you. I'd just like to sleep with you in my arms."

Enchanted, she could only nod. There was a strange, sleepy comfort in helping each other undress and coming together beneath the sheets. But he was as good as his word. Wrapping his long, lean body around her, his chest to her back, he held her close and warm until they both slept.

SHE WOKE TO the smell of coffee and Stephen's tender kiss, which she returned with languorous desire. But when he released her and she opened her eyes, she discovered he was dressed in his painting clothes.

"May I hustle you to the rose garden? One more sitting should see that portrait all but finished."

Somewhat disappointed not to be ravished, she tried not to pout. "I have the wrong clothes with me. You will have to allow me time to go back to my rooms and change. I'll meet you in the rose garden."

"You are wonderful."

Still, he sat on the bed for two minutes while she took a few sips of coffee and then dressed. She liked the way he watched her, loved the way his eyes clouded with desire. It entered her head, then, that he was being considerate because the day before and the night before had been full of physical loving. He was giving her time to recover.

The knowledge of such unprecedented care stunned her through the posing session in the rose garden, and even through breakfast with the excited Basil. Stephen agreed with Mr. Flowers to give Basil a first drawing lesson to begin the day. Aline kept her distance, sitting instead with her correspondence, her heart swelling with pride in them both.

"You can meet us in the gardens for luncheon if you like," she offered casually as Stephen took his leave. A smile of understanding passed between them, and her body went boneless with the anticipation of spending another afternoon of bliss in Stephen's arms.

How many more? she wondered. A letter from a friend informed her that the Monteignes had left town, so it was probably safe to go home. And Stephen was finishing his portraits. She had one, maybe two more days with him here at Renwick's. And then what?

She was being greedy. When what she had was not enough, surely it was time to end the affair before it became any more difficult. And yet she could not think of ending it. Trying to concentrate on her letters, an insidious voice seeped into her mind.

You love him. This time, you really, truly have found love.

But that made no sense. She liked him. She desired him. He was an interesting man and a lover to die for, sensitive and passionate and strong. But she had known him so short a time. Love was a mere fantasy inspired by being so much in each other's company. When she returned to London, she would not miss him.

I will miss him. I do love him.

Her mind kept slipping back to these circular arguments, through Basil's lessons and even when Mr. Flowers and the footmen accompanied him to find his friends for football before lunch. When she realized she had been staring at the same sentence for ten minutes and seeing only Stephen's face, she gave up and pushed the letter aside.

I am not some silly chit of a schoolgirl, she told herself severely, jumping to her feet and asking Burton for her pelisse. *A schoolgirl with a crush on her damned drawing master. Stephen and I are adults indulging in a little mutual pleasure. When our time is past, we will part as easily as we came together.*

Keep telling yourself that, Aline.

Oh God, what am I going to do?

Fastening her pelisse and pinning on the matching hat, she swung out of the room and left the hotel to watch Basil play football. It was not yet time to meet Stephen, but she could stay indoors no longer.

The boys were playing in the same meadow as yesterday, and as well as cheering children, seemed to have attracted several adult watchers. Some looked like hotel guests, others might have been local laborers or travelers from the cheaper side of the hotel.

Basil was clearly having a lovely time, haring all over the pitch set up between two sets of coats for goalposts. Aline was glad to see his guardians doing their jobs, too, moving unobtrusively up and down the sides of the unofficial pitch so that one of them at least was always within easy reach of him. They also kept an eye on their fellow watchers, and so nodded to Aline when she arrived.

Aline strolled around the perimeter of the game, thinking how good it was to see Basil playing with other children, holding shouted conversations and laughing with them. It was all very egalitarian—apart from the number of adults surreptitiously watching over Basil—and natural. And when Basil scored a goal, her heart almost burst with pride.

That was when one of the laborers brushed past to stand right in front of her. Irritated by the rudeness, she stepped around him only to find another large man planted there, too. And then they both stepped back, forcing her to do likewise.

"Your pardon, good sirs," she said sharply. "Please pay attention to where you are walking and stand aside."

They both turned then, looking not apologetic but threatening and quite unafraid. Aline had met men like that before, and she had learned never to back down.

"Really, gentlemen?" she drawled. "Going to *plant me a facer* before all these witnesses?" In fact, she was poised to act before it came to that, but their next move took her by complete surprise. They took an arm each and her reticule, containing her useful dagger, nearly fell from her wrist.

Saving it lost her valuable time, for the men simply hauled her backward away from the game, lifting her right off her feet. And they didn't let go. She was behind the other watchers now, and it was past time to act. She let her arms go limp, so that her feet sagged to the ground, and then stamped hard on one man's instep.

Even as he grunted with pain and turned furiously toward her, she brought her knee up sharply. It would have disabled him entirely except his friend upset her balance by hauling her to one side and her knee struck off-center. As it were, he let out a howl of rage and limped.

"Dennis!" she shouted to the nearest footman, for it had all happened so quickly that her own people, concentrating on Basil, hadn't even noticed.

At her call, both Dennis and Mr. Flowers looked over and as

one charged toward her. The men abducting her dragged her faster toward the wood, while she used her feet and elbows to score several hits that only slowed them down very slightly.

Behind Mr. Flowers and Dennis, the other footman, William, pounded across the pitch after her, too.

Aline finally managed to get her foot hooked around the ankle of the man to the right and yanked, tripping him flat on his face.

By then, Mr. Flowers and Dennis were almost upon them. Her attacker still standing didn't even look at his friend. He just took off into the trees. Dennis hared past her after him while Mr. Flowers threw himself on top of the tripped one who had been trying to rise.

And that was when, on the football pitch, she saw a well-dressed man take Basil by the arm. He went willingly enough, but the blood sang in her ears, pounding in time with her heart.

She was already flying across the ground toward Basil as she yelled, "It was a ruse! They're after Basil!" They had drawn his guardians away by pretending to take her. William at least should have stayed with Basil, but it was instinct to save someone under attack, and no one else seemed to have paid her any attention.

They attended now, getting smartly out of the way of the demented woman charging and leaping across the ground, keeping parallel with Basil and the man who marched him toward a gate to the road. Where a carriage and four horses awaited.

"Basil, wait!" she yelled, and at last he looked to the side and saw her. He stopped dead, and when his abductor tried to urge him on, he fought him. *Good boy, slow him down, just a few more moments...*

Behind her, she knew Mr. Flowers and the footmen were following, but sheer panic had lent her feet wings. She had never run so fast in her life.

Basil, however, was no match for a grown man who yanked him roughly onward. Someone else held the gate open and slammed it as she approached. She didn't even slow to unlatch it but gathered her skirts and leapt over it, coming to land right beside the carriage.

"Mama!" Basil clung with desperate little fingers to the side of the carriage door, while two men she knew very well tried to push him inside the carriage.

Philippe Monteigne snatched him under his arm and hauled him into the carriage. Gaston threw himself in after them and the horses began to move forward even before the door was closed. As Gaston reached for it, she jumped, landing on the coach floor, and the door slammed shut behind her.

"Mama!" From the seat, Basil dropped onto the floor beside her. Aline rose enough to clutch him to her, and over his shoulder, panting with her exertions, she glared at her first husband's uncle and cousin.

"Tie her hands," Philippe said mildly. "And do it quickly."

STEPHEN WAS PLEASED with his morning's work. His paintings bade fair to be most things that he had wanted of them. With just a few more adjustments, they could be good. Really good. Possibly the best he had ever done.

And now it was time to go and see Aline again, and that prospect, even in company with her son and other people, sent his pulses racing with happiness. Since coming to Renwick's, his life seemed to have changed quite drastically. He had come contentedly pursuing a career that was becoming successful. It was all he had truly wanted of life.

And now there was Aline, and everything was suddenly sharper. Emotions, observations, desires. As though, at last, he had come fully alive. He wanted Aline in his life. And Basil. He wanted to take on her quarrel with Basil's family, protect her, and make her happy.

But that was in the future. Things were already moving too fast between them. Not that he would have it any other way. He grinned to himself as he threw off his painting shirt and reached for his coat.

Time for a little luncheon and to hear all about Basil's football game. And Aline, Aline, Aline...

Striding toward the door, he saw a folded piece of paper on the floor in front of it. Had he been so lost in his work that he hadn't heard a knock? He bent and picked it up, hoping he had not missed Aline.

It was addressed to Mr. Dornan.

My dear Mr. Dornan,

I have been called away suddenly. No doubt we shall meet again someday.

Aline Hagerin.

He found he was sitting on the floor while the note fluttered from his hands.

Just like that, his hopes and dreams—his love—were thrown into the breeze. Leaving nothing.

CHAPTER TEN

"I DIDN'T REALLY mean you to join us, Aline," Philippe de Monteigne said sadly.

"Clearly," Aline replied from the bench opposite, where Gaston had hauled her. She had been far too exhausted by her mad run to put up more than token resistance when he had bound her hands behind her back and draped a traveling cloak about her shoulders, no doubt to conceal the oddity from any casual observers.

Basil, looking fierce and angry, sat beside her now, though he had been warned that if he tried to untie her, he would be separated from her.

"Where are we going?" she asked.

"Harwich."

"Then you mean to abduct Basil to France," she said flatly. "Do you really think the authorities will not interfere when two Frenchmen drag an English boy and his screaming mother aboard any vessel, be it a private yacht or the scheduled packet?"

Philippe smiled infinitesimally. "The boy might sound English, but he is as French as I am, and I have papers to prove it. As for you, my dear, you have no papers and *sound* as French as I am."

"Only when I choose to," Aline said in perfect, ladylike English accents.

Philippe shrugged. "Either way, you are merely a hysterical woman with no say whatever in the upbringing of your son."

Squashing the panic rising once more, she quoted carelessly, "*The law is such an ass*, it seems." She sat back on the bench, wondering if she could, with bound hands, get her fingers into the reticule still dangling from her wrist and find her dagger. "But you are going to such trouble, uncle, that I can only assume you need Basil's presence. Is the government trying to take Langterre from you?"

"From your son," Philippe retorted. "So, you needn't sound so smug about it."

"No, there's more than that," she said with certainty. And laughed. "Of course. There are moves to take Langterre from the control of a Bonapartist family, without the presence of the heir of the hero who fought against the emperor."

"Then you will recognize my determination, madam."

"I recognize your theft and your villainy. And you fail to recognize that Basil and I have friends even now coming to our rescue. I hope you hired plenty of bravos, for the two who served as your distraction will be out of action."

"They served their purpose," Philippe said complaisantly. "As for your so-called friends—I assume you mean your servants. Supposing they do anything at all beyond look for other positions, by the time they get your carriage ready, drawn by a mere two horses, they will be so far behind us that they won't matter. And we have booked ahead to change horses and even spend the night. You are outsmarted, my dear. And if you don't want to be abandoned in a ditch in the middle of nowhere, I suggest you accept the fact."

I accept nothing, she thought savagely. Though saying so was hardly in her best interests. Things were bleak, but two major assets stood in her favor. Firstly, the Monteignes had no idea what she was capable of. And if the others failed her—which she doubted—Stephen Dornan would not.

Except she did not like the amusement on Philippe's face.

"You are thinking of your most recent conquest? The painter fellow—Dornan? I wouldn't bother. We clipped his wings from the start from sending him your conge. One fewer of your knights to deal with."

STEPHEN DIDN'T KNOW how long he sat there on the floor in utter misery. He didn't want even to see her letter, but eventually, he forced himself to pick it up and read it again, in case he had missed something.

Dear Mr. Dornan. Very formal, though no doubt it achieved the distance she had intended. It was certainly written in a firm, determined hand, without hesitation or the shakiness of grief. Rather a masculine hand.

He frowned suddenly, trying to recall what he had seen of her handwriting. She had never written to him, but he had stood at her desk while a half-written epistle lay before her.

He sat up straighter, aware that he was clutching at straws, yet unable to stop himself. Even if she had made the sudden decision to part from him, would she not have made reference to their appointed meeting at luncheon? Would she really have dragged Basil away from his football game?

So little of the situation made sense that he felt more than justified in going in search of her. And if she wasn't in her rooms, he would go to the meadow because he was damned sure Basil would still be there.

Stuffing the note into his pocket, he sprang up and stalked out of his room and down to hers, where he rapped smartly on the door.

Almost immediately, it was wrenched open by Flowers.

"Dornan," he growled.

Stephen ducked beneath his blocking arm and entered the sitting room. Nearly all her servants were there—her maid, Ellen

94

the nursery maid, and Dennis the footman. Even a burly coachman that he had never seen before. They all looked beside themselves with fear and anxiety, which brought Stephen to a sudden halt.

"What?" he demanded ominously. "Where is the princess?"

"Funnily enough," Flowers said, with enough threat in his voice to scare an army, "we hoped *you* might be able to tell us."

"I?" Stephen frowned.

"You appeared in her life from nowhere, all but took it over, and now she is abducted by people who were clearly aware of her habits and protection."

"*Abducted?* Dear God! And Basil?"

"With her."

Stephen dragged the note from his pocket and slapped it on the arm of the nearest chair. "Is that her handwriting?" he demanded of Flowers.

The tutor snatched it up. "Not remotely. So, you were being kept out of the way, too."

"Tell me what happened," Stephen ordered.

He listened carefully to every detail, his heart aching and his pride in her swelling, forcing himself to think beyond his fear for them both.

"So, the carriage traveled *away* from London?" he said at last.

"We don't know which direction it took at the crossroads," Dennis said. "William's gone to see if he can discover. And John here had the horses put to the princess's carriage, so we're ready to go after them."

"But they have a coach and four and they've planned this..." Stephen was interrupted by William the footman all but falling through the door.

"They've gone north," he gasped, collapsing into the nearest chair.

"Then we'd better get after them," Flowers said grimly, striding for the door.

"Wait," Stephen said, his mind racing. "They're traveling in a coach and four, so there will be faster ways to catch them up, to pre-empt..." He began to pace because it was the only way to think and not let himself be rushed into action. "From what you say, whoever took them was really after Basil. Who would do such a thing to a child and why?"

"The ruffian I sat on said a Frenchman hired him," Flowers said. "I didn't believe him."

"Monteigne," Stephen said softly. "This is what she feared, that the Monteignes would take Basil. In which case, they're headed for France."

"Then why go north?" Flowers demanded.

Stephen paused in his pacing. "North and east. Harwich. Or some other, smaller port on the Essex coast."

"Likely," Flowers agreed, "but we cannot be sure."

"No..." His voice hardened. "Nor can we be sure they won't harm her because she's superfluous to them. It's Basil they want." He drew in his breath and regarded the coachman. "Take the carriage and follow the road to Harwich, keeping an eye out for her on the road and at the coaching inns. Dennis and William will go with you. While Mr. Flowers and I..."

"Walk?" Flowers asked, impatiently sardonic.

"No, ride. Friends of mine keep good riding horses not far from here, *and* at most of the posting inns. I'm sure one of them will have something up to your weight."

"Will they give the horses over to you?" Flowers asked dubiously.

"Oh yes," Stephen said. "If you've pistols or other weapons, bring them. Now, let's go and fetch the princess."

DESPITE ALINE'S PLANS, the carriage made good time. Neither she nor Basil were allowed to leave the carriage when the horses were changed. Gaston even held a pistol beneath his cloak, pointed directly at her to discourage her from shouting about abduction. She thought seriously about screaming anyway, just to hold things up and embroil them in a mess with the authorities. But it struck her that Gaston might just shoot her anyway and bolt for a ship to France. She would be no use to Basil then. In fact, seeing his mother shot would damage him horribly...

So, she bided her time, until darkness began to fall some distance beyond Brentwood. It had appalled her to guess they were making for Harwich, for Stephen and the others, if they discovered the Monteignes' involvement, would surely look for her in the southern ports. Dover or Southampton...

But what had Phillipe meant when he had said they'd clipped Stephen's wings? Had they hurt him? Fear for him added to everything else, and she had to fight to remain focused on the present task.

This time, when they turned into an inn yard, she made her position plain. Basil had been taken out once to relieve himself by the roadside, but he was wriggling again.

"I insist you allow us refreshment and food," she said. "If you don't, I shan't answer for the consequences. Trust me, it will not make the rest of your journey pleasant."

"And if we simply tip you out of the coach?" Gaston said.

"Then I'll have the hue and cry after you so fast you'll never get as far as a port. Besides," she added, holding Gaston's angry gaze with her calm one, "you and André were friends once. Would you really be so cruel to his widow? And don't imagine Basil would forget."

Gaston's eyes fell.

Philippe swore beneath his breath. "We'll stop here for dinner. It's off the beaten track, so we'd be safe enough staying the night. With an early start, we'll still make Harwich for the afternoon crossing."

"You'll sleep?" Gaston demanded. "With *her* in the house?"

"Yes." Philippe smiled. "Because Basil will be with me, and her door will be locked."

It was less than she had hoped but better than not stopping at all.

Annoyingly, they did not untie her hands, but kept the cloak about her, while Gaston all but lifted her from the carriage and kept his arm about her, falsely solicitous. Philippe kept Basil's hand through his arm, though the boy scowled so furiously, Aline felt rather proud of him.

The party was shown at once into a private parlor, although the innkeeper explained, wringing his hands apologetically, that he only had two bedchambers available, rather than the three Philippe requested.

Gaston looked speculatively at Aline.

"No," she said flatly. "After the day I have had, I insist on a chamber of my own. You gentlemen may all share the one room."

In fact, she didn't much care, for she sincerely hoped she would have found a means of escape before then. But Philippe took it as a sign of her acceptance of the situation and relaxed slightly. More fool him.

"They are both good-sized rooms, sirs, madam," the innkeeper said anxiously. "I can easily put up a truckle bed for the young master here. And your baggage, sir"

"Will follow with my man," Philippe lied smoothly. "Hopefully before we retire."

"Of course."

"Are the rooms ready?" Aline inquired. "I would like to see mine now."

"Of course, madam. I'll have my wife show you up immediately."

"She might as well show us all at the same time," Philippe said. He was not a complete fool, and Aline had not truly expected to win so soon.

But she would at least be granted a few minutes alone.

The innkeeper's cheery wife showed them their bedchambers on the floor above. Annoyingly, they were right beside each other. And at the front of the house, as Philippe discovered when he took it upon himself to inspect her room and peer out of the window. She already knew it was a sheer drop to the ground, although she could probably manage it if her hands were untied. She hoped it wouldn't come to that.

In the few minutes of solitude she was granted behind the closed door, she used the chamber pot and the washbowl with great difficulty, and managed, by wriggling her back against the bed, to grasp the reticule and draw it open. She even managed to reposition the dagger within for easy access, but voices in the hall warned her she was about to be interrupted. She rose to her feet, scrunching the reticule closed, and positioned it where she could easily grasp it with her left hand. Then she shook her cloak back around her and sailed out of the room.

Philippe had been quite right that she would not run without Basil.

So, they all returned together to the private parlor, Gaston holding her arm in case her balance was upset. She thought quite seriously about upsetting his. A well-timed swipe at his ankles would send him tumbling downstairs and, in the confusion, it was possible she and Basil could escape, run to the stables and steal a horse. The trouble was, she needed her hands free to have a decent chance, and Gaston was as likely to tumble into Basil as into Philippe.

Her best hope was during dinner.

In the parlor, the table had been set and a bottle of wine was placed on the sideboard along with a mug of small beer. Philippe sniffed the beer, then passed it with some distaste to Basil before he poured wine into two glasses and cocked an eye at Aline.

"Wine, *ma fille?*" he asked.

"Thank you." She watched him pour a third glass and sat down at one end of the table. "My hands?" she pointed out.

Philippe considered her. "That is a problem," he said, placing the glass in front of her. After which, he sat down to her left.

Swine.

Basil set down his small beer after one swallow and stalked up to her. Lifting the glass, he held it to her lips and let her drink. Over the rim, she held his gaze and closed one eye. Basil's face lightened, and he set down the glass, taking the seat on her other side.

If the inn staff thought it odd she still wore the traveling cloak when they brought in the dinner, they said nothing. After all, to them, this party was foreign and therefore strange and probably heathen.

"Just leave the dishes," Philippe commanded. "We shall serve ourselves."

They bowed themselves out, no doubt shaking their heads on the other side of the door. Gaston served everyone soup.

"One free hand would be helpful," Aline pointed out. "I wouldn't like to upset your digestion by slurping from the bowl like a dog."

"I cannot imagine you sacrificing your dignity," Philippe replied, raising his spoon to his mouth. "But your hands will remain as they are."

Beside her, Basil let out an exclamation of outrage, glaring at his great uncle who, however, held Aline's gaze blandly and carried on eating, as did Gaston.

"You never used to be cruel, Philippe," she observed. "I wonder what André would think of you now?"

"André!" Philippe all but dropped his spoon in his sudden irritation. "André lost all sense when he married you! You took him away from us, turned him against his family, his country—"

"You misjudge him if you think I could influence him to that degree. He was against neither his family nor his country, only Bonaparte when he named himself emperor. And he never ever lost his human decency. A lesson there, I think, gentlemen."

"Basil, feed your mother," Philippe said. "At least it might stop her talking."

"Saying things you don't wish to hear." Gracefully, Aline accepted a spoonful of soup from her son. The role reversal was meant to humiliate her, but she made the most of it, reminding Basil how she had used to feed him by pretending the spoon was a bird flying across the sky to deposit food in his mouth. He even smiled, doing the same for her, and thus it was a game.

It was also a distraction. While Basil fed her morsels of food in between his own mouthfuls, she loosened her hold of the reticule dangling from her left wrist and once more inserted the fingers of her right hand and managed to grasp the dagger. It took some time, but she eventually got it out of the reticule and maneuvered the blade against the rope.

She actually had to hold the dagger by the blade with the fingers of her right hand, which was both dangerous and painful. And still, she had to eat and focus overtly on Basil, who played the silly feeding game like a younger child, as though he knew she was up to something and was joining in to help.

Her heart swelled as she worked and planned and played. And among all that concentration on so many activities, something else slipped into her mind, half recognition, half pure emotion.

Stephen Dornan was worth fighting for. She had known he was different from the first time she had met him, and that difference was love. Lasting, powerful, overwhelming love. It did not fight her maternal love. It absorbed it, shared it. And so, she cared nothing for the cuts on her fingers or the raw chafing of the ropes, because she would do anything to save Basil and return to Stephen.

He might never love her the same way. But she would try, and she would do her best to win him and make him happy... She could have a proper family, safety, security for herself and Basil...

But first, she had to get out of here.

A piece of apple tart was pushed in front of her. Again, Basil fed her a forkful before beginning his own. The Monteignes were looking sour, as if annoyed that she had defeated humiliation. And with one last minute saw of the blade, the rope was cut.

It was such a relief she had to fight to keep her hands in place, to keep hold of the blade that become slick with blood. Her fingers shook as she changed position, holding the dagger by it its hilt and waiting for the trembling to stop.

Two, three more pieces of apple tart, carefully taken and chewed and swallowed, and then she pushed back her chair, as though finally impatient.

"I've had enough, Basil. Eat your own," she said.

She pushed to her feet. "Am I to sleep like this as well?" she demanded.

Philippe smiled, the moron, as she paced behind him. "Sadly, yes."

"Wrong," she said and shrugged off the cloak. In almost the same movement, her arm snaked around Philippe's neck and the dagger pricked at his throat. "Not one move, uncle, or I shall be forced to upset my son further."

Basil had dropped his fork, staring at her hand. "B-blood, Mama!"

"My fingers will heal," she said soothingly, while the dagger pricked more significantly at Philippe's skin, saying the unspoken words for her. *Your throat will not heal.*

As though released from paralysis, Gaston leapt to his feet, knocking over his chair. "Papa!"

He lunged toward his father, who yelped, "Be still, you fool!" Just as the parlor door burst open, and Stephen Dornan walked in, Mr. Flowers close at his heels.

"Stand and deliver," Stephen said cheerfully into the sudden silence. He held a pistol that swung to aim straight at Gaston's heart.

Aline wanted to laugh and cry and scream all the same time. Instead, she said shakily, "What kept you?"

He smiled directly into her eyes, a quick, dazzling glance before his gaze returned to Gaston. "What kept us? Finding a horse large enough to carry Flowers. And then we misjudged how far you would travel. We meant to catch you on the road, hence *Stand and deliver*, which I've always wanted to say and refused to give up."

Was he *babbling?* Stephen Dornan? He really had been worried for her. Warmth spread through her like a gently glowing fire. But they were not yet out of the woods.

"He has a pistol," she said. "Gaston. It's in his pocket, I think. *That* is Gaston, my first husband's cousin. This is his uncle, Philippe."

"Hands slowly in the air, Cousin Gaston," Stephen said.

She had never heard his voice so cold, so implacable. Yet another side of the man she would never tire of discovering. Gaston, far more nervous than his father, obeyed at once.

"Mr. Flowers?" Stephen suggested, and the tutor, without further instruction, marched up to Gaston, keeping well clear of Stephen's line of fire at all times. The pistol was located without trouble and withdrawn. Mr. Flowers pocketed it and strolled away.

"Basil," Stephen said steadily. "Would you be so good as to go to Mr. Flowers?"

Basil stood but hesitated, his wide gaze on Aline. "Mama," he uttered uncertainly, clearly unhappy to leave her anywhere near Philippe.

"I'm coming," she assured him. "The instant after I assure Uncle Philippe that I can throw the dagger, too."

Encouraged, Basil walked slowly and reluctantly away from Aline to the tutor, who put his arm around the boy in a quick, hard hug.

Aline removed the dagger from Philippe's throat and stepped back.

"How badly are you hurt?" Stephen asked conversationally, without taking his eyes off Gaston.

"Barely at all. A few minor cuts to my fingers."

"I'd call him out, but he doesn't appear to be a gentleman," Stephen remarked.

"Oh, please!" Philippe said in apparent amusement. Without the knife to his throat, he had recovered his urbanity with remarkable speed. "I believe you English have a saying about pots and kettles. Aline, you have wasted your time in the last five minutes and would do well to sit down again. And to deliver Basil to Gaston, for this...*man*, this *Dornan*, will be holding the pistol on *my* instructions at any moment. He is a man prone to change sides."

Aline laughed. "How long have you been having these delusions, Philippe?" She had joined Basil and Mr. Flowers, and now they moved toward Stephen between the Monteignes and the door.

"Since I spoke to Dornan senior," Philippe said, smiling. "Did you know your knight in shining armor here is a traitor and a one-time Bonapartist? I'm sure it is also news to his ally, the tutor."

Whatever she had expected to come out of Philippe's mouth, it was not that.

"You didn't know, did you?" Philippe was definitely amused now. "But how charming! He was in France during the war, Aline, and there could only be one reason for that, one possibility that allowed him to stay among his country's enemies. He was paid by Bonaparte—for which I must applaud him, of course, though I doubt you do. He was even in Paris during the Hundred Days when the emperor was free, probably right up to Waterloo. Were you not, monsieur?"

"Yes, and after Waterloo, too," Stephen said, astonishing her further. His hand brushed against her, caught her fingers and she clung. Whatever he was about to say, she trusted him implicitly. "I traveled about Europe for several years, dodging the armies, painting where I could. Mostly in Italy, actually. Not the best time to see anywhere, really, ravaged by decades of war, but I learned a huge amount. And then I stopped off in Paris on my way home, and so I was indeed there during the Hundred Days."

"And if you do not hand me that pistol," Philippe said in suddenly freezing tones, "I will make known to everyone in your country that you were a traitor and a spy."

"I was not."

"My dear fellow, that will hardly matter when your commissions dry up and you are reduced to penury. You will be quite the pariah. Unless you give me the pistol, in which case I am inclined to forget what I know."

"But you have already misunderstood what you know," Stephen said gently. "And your so-called revelation will surprise no one. I daresay it will surprise *you*, however, to hear what *I* learned during the Hundred Days. That on the emperor's return, you accused your neighbor—a Monsieur Duclos, I believe?—of continued violence in the cause of the Bourbon king, that you had him arrested and summarily executed, just so that you could increase your landholding. One could call it patriotic except it wasn't remotely true, was it? Duclos was an inoffensive old man, whose family had been farming those few acres and keeping their noses out of politics for generations. The accusation was purely malicious, but he still died, and I very much doubt *your* friends and neighbors will approve of *that*."

"Jesu, how do you know it was us?" Gaston blurted.

Philippe scowled at him.

"Duclos," Aline whispered on a rush of memory and shame and grief. "You had M. Duclos executed? Dear God, for a few paltry acres..."

"How did I know?" Stephen repeated. "I couldn't quite remember myself why I knew your name, and then I recalled. It was on certain documents that passed through my hands. During the Hundred Days."

He moved the pistol's aim from Gaston to Philippe. "So, here is what will happen, gentlemen. You will leave the inn *now*, and travel through the night to Harwich, where you will take a ship for France. You will never trouble the princess or Basil again. And you will vacate Basil's estate exactly when she requires you to. If you do not comply, if you are ever even *seen* in the British Isles again, I will make sure certain documents are placed before the *current* French authorities. And now, monsieur, you should be on your way."

CHAPTER ELEVEN

A s SOON AS the door closed behind the Monteignes, Aline
sagged against Stephen, reaching blindly for Basil with her
other hand, and hugging him convulsively.

"My brave boy," she whispered and tried to laugh up at Stephen and the stolidly watching Mr. Flowers. "All my brave boys!
My formal thanks for the rescue, gentlemen."

"You seemed to have matters well under control," Stephen
said with unmistakable pride. Was that his lips brushing against
her hair?

"We might have had more problems actually getting out of
the inn," Aline admitted. "And now we don't need to because you
sent them away instead. I can't believe I trusted them with Basil
only a few months ago."

"Desperation makes people greedy," Stephen offered.

"I'll make sure they actually go," Flowers growled, heading
for the door.

"And order supper," Aline called after him. "You and Stephen
must be starving."

But as Mr. Flowers left, the innkeeper, his wife, and one of
the maids leapt back from the door. They had clearly been trying
to listen, to work out if it was safe to enter. They parted like the
Red Sea for Flowers, and Stephen said, "Some clean water and
bandages in here if you please."

Aline, who had dealt with much worse alone, found it rather lovely to be cossetted and cared for. Stephen led her to a seat at the table, pushing crockery aside to make space for the bowl of water and the box of bandages and salves brought by the maid. Then, he knelt at her feet and began to clean her hands and wrists. His lips tightened as his fingertips brushed over the rope marks on her wrist. He was thorough and gentle, and for the first time since she had been attacked outside Renwick's Hotel, she felt like weeping.

"Will Mama be well?" Basil asked shakily.

"Of course, I will," she exclaimed, though he seemed to need to hear it from Stephen.

"Yes, she will be fine," Stephen said. "Her wrists and hands will be sore and stingy for a little, but nothing is deep. Now, tell me everything."

Halfway through Aline and Basil's joint account of their adventure, which had the added bonus of making it all seem fun to Basil now he was safe, Mr. Flowers returned.

"They've gone as if all the fiends of hell are after them. By a piece of good luck, William and Dennis drove up and spilled out of the carriage, looking furious and menacing, and supervised their departure."

Stephen grinned. So did Basil.

"They send their good wishes, ma'am. And are relieved to know you and Basil are safe."

"Spoiling for a fight, were they?" Stephen asked.

"I wouldn't have been able to hold them back if I hadn't assured them you were both safe."

"They are good men," Aline said warmly. "And you, Mr. Flowers, are an incomparable tutor.

"Do you want to know what happened to us, too?" Basil said eagerly, and so the rest of the tale was told, while more wine was opened, and the table re-covered with food. And then Stephen and Mr. Flowers told their story, too, and Stephen showed her the note purporting to come from her.

She stared at it. "But that's... Why in the world...? How did they even know...?"

"My father, apparently," Stephen said ruefully. "They'd clearly spoken to him, for they said he'd told them I was in France. He must have also told them you were my reason for staying at Renwick's."

"Monteigne must have thought it a good way of reducing the number of your protectors," Mr. Flowers said.

"Did you believe it?" Aline asked Stephen curiously.

"For a little," he admitted. "Until my brain kicked in and I realized the abrupt little note didn't sound like you at all. So, I went down to your rooms and found everyone in an uproar over your and Basil's abduction."

"Dennis discovered the direction of their carriage," Mr. Flowers said, "and we concluded they were making for Harwich. We sent William and Dennis to follow in the carriage, in case they found you on the way, while Dornan and I came on horseback."

"Calton's horses," Dornan explained. "I hope he doesn't need them in a hurry."

"We almost went straight past this inn," Mr. Flowers said. "But decided to ask in passing before riding on. And the staff were so wary of the foreign gents and the lady who ate in her traveling cloak as if she didn't want her skirts to touch their furniture, that we knew you were here. Offered to sort you all out."

Aline smiled wryly. "I shall be sure never to wear the wretched cloak inside the inn again."

"Oh, they all know you were under duress," Mr. Flowers assured her. "The innkeeper's wife is as furious as the rest of us and will probably board you for nothing. Talking of boarding..."

"We have two bedrooms," Basil piped up. "I was supposed to stay with the nasty uncles, and Mama was to sleep with her wrists bound behind her back!"

"Well, we certainly won't have that," Aline said stoutly. "You can sleep in my room now."

"Could I not stay with Mr. Flowers and Mr. Dornan?" Basil

asked. "That would be a better end to a manly adventure!"

"True," Aline said, trying not to feel hurt.

Stephen refilled her wine glass. "We should have brought your maid along with Dennis and William."

"I can do without her for a night or two."

There was admiration in Stephen's eyes. Her independence, her past, her use of a dagger that most ladies would scream at the sight of, none of that appalled him. With a fresh surge of longing, she wondered if he saw beneath those things, to her yearning for peace and security and love.

⫸⫷

STEPHEN WAS APPALLED. By the injuries she had sustained to free herself, by the awful possibilities of what might have happened. It brought her sheer capability and the dangers she had overcome in her past into sharp focus. He was proud, admiring, fascinated—and terrified.

While Basil slept peacefully in the truckle bed, Stephen and Flowers sat on the window seat of their bedchamber, sharing a last glass of brandy and talking desultorily.

"If only she had waited for us," Stephen said into the silence, trying to make sense of his thought, "she would not have hurt herself."

"I don't think we could have come much faster, without the risk of missing them." Flowers glanced at him. "Was that your point?"

"No, my point is that she hurt herself."

"The scars will fade," Flowers said deliberately, "if that is your concern."

Stephen shifted restlessly. "Scars fade," he repeated. "They don't all go away... Though perhaps they cease to hurt."

Flowers sipped his brandy. He seemed to know Stephen was not still talking about physical wounds. "She looked at you very oddly when Monteigne revealed you were in Paris."

"I was not betraying my country," Stephen said mildly.

"I know that. So does she. But *you* knew what the Monteignes had done. *She* did not. Is that not worthy of more explanation than the reasons she did not sit back and wait to be rescued by people she had no idea were coming?"

Stephen stared at him. "Dear God, I'm not criticizing her, Flowers. I *fear* for her!"

Flowers shrugged. "It comes with the territory."

"What territory?" Stephen scowled.

"Besottedness," Flowers replied. "It seems to me you should be deciding whether you want to live with that or without it."

Stephen closed his eyes, letting his head fall back against the windowpane.

"I see," Flowers said. "Then I have two things to say to you. Firstly, if you ever hurt a hair on her head or betray her in the smallest way, I will break your legs. Secondly, what the hell are you doing here with me?"

Stephen's eyes flew open, his breath catching on sudden, devastating clarity. With a sound between a laugh and a growl, he sprung to his feet and handed Flowers his glass. "I'll let you."

"Let me what?"

"Break my legs if I betray her."

RETIRING TO BED alone with her hands free and her son safe, held a certain sort of contentment. And yet part of her wished they could have all have simply fallen asleep in the inn parlor, in the comforting camaraderie that had prevailed once the Monteignes were sent about their business.

Another part of her wished Stephen was here with her. The innkeeper's wife had unfastened her gown and stays and made a fuss over her. But lying in bed, exhausted, Aline could not sleep.

Because Stephen was not here. Because she did not know what he thought of her now or even what she wanted him to think. She did not know how he knew about the Monteignes' betrayal of Duclos, something she hadn't known herself, and suspicions chased themselves around her brain, alternately hopeful and anxious.

She had entirely given up on sleep and on his company when a faint scratch sounded at the door. She sat up and lit the lamp. By its pale light, she saw the door opening and the figure that stepped through, swiftly closing it behind him again.

"Aline. It's Stephen. May I come in?"

"You are in."

"So I am." He came toward her, quick, decisive, yet surely without his usual confidence. Had he come to end it? Whatever *it* was that had sprung between them so quickly, so consumingly— at least for her.

Her heart skittered as the lamplight played across the fine angles of his face, and he sank down on the bed, twisting around to face her.

Slowly, as if afraid she would stop him, he took her bandaged hands in his and raised one to his cheek. "I hate that you're injured. I hate that I could not prevent it."

"I think you've prevented it happening again," she said lightly.

"I need to tell you something."

Don't leave me. Please don't leave me. Somehow, she held his gaze. "I know."

He drew in a breath. "I think... I think I was the man in the Paris garret who passed your information to various smugglers and officers of the Royal Navy. The man you thought you betrayed."

She swallowed, wondering if she could bear it. "What happened to you?"

"Nothing," he said, softly kissing her bandages. "I was away, at the coast, and when I returned, the street was too quiet, too

111

watchful. I didn't go in. I found somewhere else to stay. And then there was Waterloo. The point is, you betrayed no one. Even if they had arrested me, it would not have been your fault. Any fault was mine then. As it is mine now. I should have told you as soon as I suspected. I should not have let you suffer, just because I wasn't sure. Receiving the documents, from you and others, was just something I fell into, something I felt obliged to do to prevent yet more war in Europe. And something I quickly forgot about again. I never thought of anyone *worrying* about me."

Her hand moved in his, and he released it at once. But she reached up, touching his cheek, his lips with two unbandaged, unhurt fingertips.

"Not enough people have worried about you in your life, Stephen Dornan," she whispered achingly. "I would like your permission to worry about you, to care for you, because I shall do it anyway."

He smiled, his curved lips brushing her fingertips. His voice was not quite steady as he said, "I was about to say the same to you." He leaned toward her, giving her time to avoid him, but she only parted her lips to receive his kiss, sweet and tender.

"I am dancing about this," he whispered against her lips. "Because I am afraid it is too quick, afraid it will drive you away. Don't let it. I don't ask for anything in return."

"In return for what?"

"I love you." He touched the side of her face, and only then did she realize it was damp.

"Oh, Stephen, come to bed," she whispered brokenly.

He did, and it didn't take long. He had come to her without his boots or his coat, so he removed everything else in moments, and slid into bed beside her. She reached for him at once, and he kissed her foolish tears, her eyelids, her lips. His arms were strong and safe around her, his long, lean body warm and increasingly aroused.

"You need to sleep, Aline," he murmured. "Let me hold you while you sleep."

"That would be lovely," she said honestly. "But would you make love to me first?"

There was relief as well as pleasure in his smiling eyes as he covered her mouth with his. Despite his own desire, the need she sensed barely contained beneath his surface courtesy, he would have let her sleep and that touched her almost as much as the stunning fact that he loved her.

He drew her shift slowly up over her hips and waist and breasts until he could tug it right over her head and throw it aside. His kisses, his wonderful, sensitive hands traveled all over her body, arousing and thrilling.

It was a slow, gentle loving that yet seemed to reach into her soul. Sheer emotion tangled with the physical pleasures until they became one and the same. In the whole world, there seemed to be only her and Stephen, joined together, moving in languorous tender strokes. Even as the ecstasy built and built, to unendurable intensity, he did not rush. And when it broke, he held her there while she moaned and gasped and held on to him.

"Stay," she pleaded, "Stay with me. I love you..." And with a soft groan, he gave in, releasing the tide of his own joy while hers surged yet again, and they collapsed together in a welter of sheets and tears and utter happiness.

⤜⤜⤜⟫⟫⟫

"WILL YOU MARRY me, Aline?" he asked her, just before he fell asleep. He felt boneless and ecstatic after their loving, and her words of love had brought him at least as much joy.

Her eyes opened, sleepily smiling, although there was a hint of worry behind it. "Unfair to ask me after that. I will agree to anything when you love me."

"That's settled then."

She laughed. "No, it isn't," she said, kissing him and closing her eyes again.

So did he, and in each other's arms, they fell asleep.

He was foolish, he knew, to expect everything at once. This night was enough for now. Her love was more than he had ever dreamed of. Beneath whatever held her back, she was already his, and he would marry her.

CHAPTER TWELVE

"D O YOU LIKE Mr. Dornan?" Aline asked Basil casually. They had been back at Renwick's Hotel for two days and were planning to leave for town that afternoon. So, she and Basil were making a last visit to the pleasure garden, which gave her a rare moment of privacy with her son, to learn Basil's views.

"Yes, I like him." Basil grinned. "He says I can call him Stephen! And he likes my drawings. Maybe mine will be as good as his one day."

"Maybe," she agreed. "Would you mind if he came to live with us?"

Stephen's eyes widened a bit. "No, that might be fun. Doesn't he have a house of his own?"

"I think he does, in the country. We could live with him there sometimes, too."

"Oh yes," Stephen enthused. "Does he have dogs and horses? And lambs?"

Aline laughed. "I expect so, though you would have to ask him. The thing is, he has asked me to marry him, and I wondered if you thought that was a good idea."

Stephen thought about it. "You're happier around him."

"Am I?" Aline asked, smiling. *Of course, I am.* "So are you, I think."

"And Mr. Flowers likes him. He doesn't glare at him anymore, except in fun. You probably should marry him. Then we can all be happy. He's not like the prince, is he?"

Aline swallowed. "No, he's not like the prince. Do you miss your stepfather?"

"Not really. He was kind enough, but he didn't really see me. I wasn't comfortable there. I like it here, though. In town. And I would like to live in the country, too. Stephen can teach me how to ride better."

"I'm sure he will."

Basil was an odd mixture of childishness and maturity, shrewdness and naivety. Perhaps all children were. His words echoed around her mind as they wandered around the entertainments and returned to the hotel to pack up the last of their things. Something had bothered her though she couldn't put her finger on what.

"Mr. Dornan was looking for you, madam," Burton said as they returned to the room. "He asked that you step up to his studio when you return."

"Very well," Aline said calmly, though, in fact, she was both surprised and pleased by the invitation. She hadn't seen a great deal of him since their return to Renwick's. Although he had dined with them each night, and taken every opportunity to befuddle her with ravishing kisses, he had been working mostly on his paintings, for which, it seemed, he no longer needed her to sit. Or was that why she had been summoned?

She made her familiar way to the room next to the staff stairs on the floor above and knocked. The door opened at once, and Stephen stood there in his shirt-sleeves, although there were no obvious signs of paint on him.

His eyes lit up at the sight of her, making her heart race, although he seemed unusually serious.

"Aline, come in. Thank you. I wanted you to see them now because I know you will be honest with me, and I am afraid of being too involved to see straight."

He closed the door behind her while she watched him warily.

"You're babbling. That means you're worried."

"Damnably worried, if you'll pardon my language. Will you look at the portraits?"

Only then did she realize he had all the easels set up with uncovered canvases. "Of course."

He took her hand and led her to the easels. And suddenly, there she was in the rose garden, a bundle of exquisite, colorful roses in her arm while she reached for a higher bloom and glanced back with an expression that betrayed both humor and hurry. Something about it made her blush.

"It's me," she blurted.

"So is this." He led her to the next, where she sat at an outside table in the sunshine, eating ice cream with an expression of innocent yet sensual bliss.

Her blush deepened. "I can never eat ice cream again."

"I hope you will," he said fervently.

Still stunned by her own likeness, she stumbled after him to the next portrait. Basil sat beside her with a piece of cake. She had sewing work in her hand, but her attention was on her son, not politely or even foolishly besotted as some people looked at their offspring, but with utter, genuine enjoyment of his company.

"That is it," she said in wonder, moving on to the next picture, where she sat on the bed, teasing and yet...seductive. And a little unsure. He had caught that. He caught everything.

Dragging her gaze free, she stared at the largest of the paintings, the one of her twirling around in the "secret" garden under the lantern light and the moonlight. She was rapt, delighted, excited, and yet content in her wonder. He had caught the movement of her swirling gown, the sheer joy of the moment, and more.

"This," she whispered as the tears threatened. "This. Oh, Stephen. Oh, Stephen," She turned into his arms and he held her.

"That bad?" he murmured ruefully into her hair.

"That good!" she retorted fiercely. "That astonishingly. They are so insightful, I almost wish they were of someone else, but then I wouldn't know…"

"Wouldn't know what?" he asked, stroking her hair with one hand while he tilted up her chin with the other.

"That you know me, that you *see* me. You have made me beautiful, but I'm me as I've never seen myself, as no one has but you… Basil said to me just a little while ago that the prince, my late husband, hadn't really seen him, and it just came to me that he hadn't really seen me either. Everyone has ideas about me, and perhaps I foster that, I hide… But you *see* me, and you love me anyway."

To stop the stream of words, she kissed him fiercely. "We see each other. We can worry for each other because we care. God, I do love you, Stephen. Will you marry me?"

Stephen's face lit up in one of those dazzling smiles she'd seen a lot more of since coming to Renwick's, but she only caught a glimpse of it before he blocked out the light and kissed her until the world was warm and dark and swirling with passion.

It was the work of moments to fall on the bed and mere minutes to release the powerful surge of emotion in the sweetest, most satisfying way.

It took a little longer to pack off Stephen's paintings to Paris, and a week or so after that to marry. They went to Paris for their wedding journey, and Aline was much feted as the model of the winning entries of the competition. Various artists and art lovers tried brazenly to entice her away from her husband. But they never stood a chance. Stephen was and remained her sole love and the only gentleman of pleasure she wanted.

About Mary Lancaster

Mary Lancaster lives in Scotland with her husband, three mostly grown-up kids and a small, crazy dog.

Her first literary love was historical fiction, a genre which she relishes mixing up with romance and adventure in her own writing. Her most recent books are light, fun Regency romances written for Dragonblade Publishing: *The Imperial Season* series set at the Congress of Vienna; and the popular *Blackhaven Brides* series, which is set in a fashionable English spa town frequented by the great and the bad of Regency society.

Connect with Mary on-line – she loves to hear from readers:

Email Mary:
Mary@MaryLancaster.com

Website:
www.MaryLancaster.com

Newsletter sign-up:
http://eepurl.com/b4Xoif

Facebook:
facebook.com/mary.lancaster.1656

Facebook Author Page:
facebook.com/MaryLancasterNovelist

Twitter:
@MaryLancNovels

Amazon Author Page:
amazon.com/Mary-Lancaster/e/B00DJ5IACI

Bookbub:
bookbub.com/profile/mary-lancaster

CPSIA information can be obtained
at www.ICGtesting.com
Printed in the USA
BVHW030825220622
640233BV00016BA/505